HUGHES

Switching tracks

SWITCHING TRACKS

SWITCHING
TRACKS

by Dean Hughes

Atheneum • 1982 • New York

Library of Congress Cataloging in Publication Data

Hughes, Dean
    Switching tracks.

    Summary: A lonely ninth grader, struggling with the
knowledge of his father's death, befriends an old man.
    [1. Loneliness—Fiction. 2. Suicide—Fiction.
3. Friendship—Fiction] I. Title.
PZ7.H87312Sw   [Fic]   82-3899
ISBN 0-689-30923-6   AACR2

Copyright © 1982 by Dean Hughes
All rights reserved
Published simultaneously in Canada by
McClelland & Stewart, Ltd.
Composition by American—Stratford Graphic Services, Inc.,
Brattleboro, Vermont
Printed and bound by Fairfield Graphics,
Fairfield, Pennsylvania
Designed by Felicia Bond
First Edition

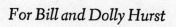

For Bill and Dolly Hurst

SWITCHING TRACKS

CHAPTER 1

IIIIIIIIIIIIIIIIIIIIIIIIIIIIIIIIIIIIIIIIIIIIIIIIIIIIIIIIIIIIIIIIIII
IIIIIIIIIIIIIIIIIIIIIIIIIIIIIIIIIIIIIIIIIIIIIIIIIIIIIIIIIIIIIIIIIII

Mark was one of the first to get on the bus, but he went almost to the back and took a seat by the window. The old bus was almost full before someone sat down by him, but the guy who did was with a couple of friends, and they took the seats just ahead. The boy next to Mark—everyone called him Whittington—leaned forward and said something to his friends, but he didn't speak to Mark. Not that it mattered. The kid was in a couple of Mark's classes, including gym, and Mark knew what a jerk he was. Whittington's big thrill in life was waiting until some guy went in the shower and then hiding his towel or throwing his gym shoes in the urinal.

Mark looked out the window toward the decaying junior high building and the clusters of kids who were still waiting outside for their buses. But he gave no thought to what he was looking at. He hated the junior high and was glad to be getting away from it for the day. He had only been going to school there for a month, just since school had started. He had moved across town during the summer and so he hardly knew anyone.

"Hey, Anders, I saw Carla talking to that high school kid—that guy we saw her with last week."

Mark glanced over at Whittington, but he didn't give much thought to what he had heard him say. Anders twisted around and made some comment, grinning all the while, but Mark turned and looked out the window again. He wished he had a dollar or two so that he could go down to the arcade when he got home. But he had spent all his money there yesterday.

He had homework to do—he had even brought the books with him—but he knew already that he wouldn't do it. Most of his classes didn't require much homework; he could pretty well bluff his way through. But he was getting behind in math. It wasn't that he didn't understand the stuff, it was just that he only did what he could get done in class. He kept intending to catch up, and his teacher had told him he could still get the work in, but once school was out each day, he could never bring himself to do it.

Whittington was saying something about Carla

again—whoever that was—and Anders and the other guy were laughing. Mark shut his eyes and leaned back against the brittle plastic, the green stuff that had been used to re-cover the old seats. He was small for an eighth-grader, and there wasn't much about him that caused anyone to notice him—or remember him. His hair was sort of colorless—more or less brown—and he wore it a little shorter than most of the guys did. He actually had rather clear blue eyes, but he had a habit of looking down when anyone looked at him. He hadn't started with pimples yet, or with the fuzzy, dirty-looking hair on his upper lip, but that was only because he hadn't started to mature. The only really distinctive thing about him was that he wore the same T-shirt to school about three days out of five. It was a ragged old tan thing that was stretched out of shape, the neck drooping lopsidedly.

The bus ride only took fifteen minutes or so. Mark sat with his eyes shut. Whittington talked most of the time, over the seat to Anders, but it was the usual stupid talk about cheating in Spanish class and punching some guy if he didn't watch his step. Whittington had a big voice, deep and sloppy, and he let his important statements fill the whole back end of the bus, but he never seemed to notice that Mark was even there.

When the bus had almost reached Mark's stop, Whittington suddenly leaned over Mark and snapped the sliding window back. "Hey, gramps," he yelled, "what're yuh doin' today?" His changing voice boomed but cracked at the end. He was a big kid, taller than most of the ninth graders, but soft, almost fat. Every day it was his ritual to yell at this old man who was usually sitting out on his porch in the afternoons. "Gramps, yuh havin' a good time? Don't kick over with a heart attack from all the excitement."

Anders slid his window back too. "Don't let this busload of girls get you all heated up, gramps. You're too old to think about stuff like that."

A few of the kids laughed. Most were preoccupied with other things. There was always a mild sort of roar on the bus, kids yelling back and forth, usually shouting insults. A never-ending stream of sarcasm passed between the girls and the boys. Mark glanced over at the old man on the porch. He showed no reaction. Didn't seem annoyed or hurt. He just stared back, almost curiously. "See yuh tomorrow, gramps," Whittington yelled. "I know this is the only thrill you get all day." He leaned back after that and continued his conversation with Anders. Mark thought the whole thing was stupid, but it had become part of the daily routine, and he didn't really pay much attention. The old man lived just four or five houses up the street from Mark, and sometimes he passed Mark on afternoon walks, but Mark didn't even know his name.

When the bus stopped, Mark was already up and waiting. He was always relieved when the ride was over. There was nothing at home, but at least he was on his own for a while. His mother didn't get home for another hour and a half, and his little brother usually spent his time with a couple of friends in the neighborhood.

Mark went in and dumped his books in the bedroom. He hated the crummy little house they had been forced to move into. Every time he looked at the worn-out carpet in his room and the yellowing wallpaper, he wanted to be home, back in the house he had grown up in. It hadn't been all that fancy either, but it had been a little bigger and a lot newer. Everything had been better then—even with all the problems his dad had caused.

But he didn't like to think about these kinds of things. He knew what it could lead to. Suddenly he felt a little panicky. Best to walk into the kitchen and look around for something to eat. He grabbed a handful of Ritz crackers out of the cabinet and then went back to his bedroom and flipped on the radio. He lay on his bed and listened to the music and ate the crackers, but he could hardly stand all the stupid things the disc jockey kept saying—and the dumb kids who kept calling in to make requests. Then a quiet song came on, gentle, with plenty of room for Mark to think, and he was afraid again. He didn't actually see the scene in his mind—not the one that had been coming so often at night lately—nor did he hear the words, but he knew that if he didn't do something quickly, he would start to see it and hear it. Especially he didn't want to hear the words. He jumped up and grabbed his basketball and headed outside. There was a hoop, without a net, bolted to the old garage out in back. It was sort of crooked and not really regulation height, but it didn't matter—he wasn't good at basketball anyway.

He took a few shots but didn't really knock himself out. Just walked over and retrieved the ball, maybe dribbled a time or two, and then took another shot. He had taken a little jump shot when he heard footsteps on the gravel driveway behind him.

Mark spun around. "Yuh missed." It was the old man—the one Whittington always yelled at. Mark didn't say anything, just walked over and got the ball. "How yuh doing?" the man said. He was a big man with lots of white hair that seemed to be turning yellow in places. He wasn't stooped or frail-looking, but his face was deeply creased, especially around the eyes, and he had big flabby-looking ears. He was wearing an old pair of striped overalls that were even more faded than the jeans Mark was wearing.

"I'm okay," Mark said. He really didn't feel like talking to the old guy.

"You going out for basketball?" The man had a gravelly voice.

"No."

"Why not?"

" 'Cause I'm no good. I couldn't make it."

"Well, I think you're probably right about that," the man said, and he laughed quietly, the air sucking between his teeth.

Mark was surprised. He turned and saw that the man was still grinning, his blunt brown teeth showing.

At least he hadn't started one of those stupid speeches about everyone being able to make it if he worked hard enough.

"Your name's Austin, isn't it?"

"Yuh," Mark said. He took another shot that hit the front of the rim and bounced away.

"I talked to your mother a couple of times. She's a very nice lady." Mark didn't answer. He got the ball and shot again, missing everything. "You're terrible," the man said. Mark found himself smiling as he went after the ball.

"Your mother said that your dad died last spring."

Mark didn't want to talk about that. "That's right," he said. He dribbled in for a lay-up, just to show the old guy that he could make one.

"I guess it's been kind of tough on you, hasn't it?"

Mark grabbed the ball and held it under his arm, then he looked at the old man straight on. "No, it hasn't. Not at all."

"Is that right?" The old man had his thumbs hooked under the straps of his overalls, like a picture of an old time farmer.

"Yes, that's right. I hardly ever saw my dad, and I didn't like him." Mark wanted to shock the guy.

But the man didn't seem to react. He nodded, quietly. "I guess that's more or less the way I felt about my old man. I left home when I wasn't much older than you are."

It was Mark who was surprised. He had never known an adult to say anything like that. It confused him for a second, and he didn't know what to reply. So he turned and took an awkward shot that went well over the basket. As he went after the ball, he could hear the man laughing again. "You *are* terrible," he said.

Mark walked back toward the basket, bouncing the ball, but he didn't shoot. "So who are *you* supposed to be—Magic Johnson?" He bounced the ball toward the man. "Let's see you put it in."

The old man grinned. He took a couple of steps forward. "I wasn't too bad once, you know," he said. He took a stiff shot that died before it ever got close to the basket. Mark laughed, but so did the man. "My name's Willard," he said, after a moment. "I was wondering if you wanted to walk down to my place for a few minutes. There's something I want to show you."

Mark was surprised again. He looked at the man and intended to say no, but then the old guy motioned to him to follow and started away. Mark held his ground for a few seconds, until the man turned around and said, "Come on. But you better leave that ball here. You could hurt someone with that thing." He was chuckling again, with his raspy voice, as he began walking away. Mark put the basketball down and followed him. Might as well find out what the heck the old guy wanted.

Willard, or Mr. Willard—Mark didn't know whether that was his first or last name—lived in a little white frame house. It needed paint, and the climbing rose bush out front had gotten out of control, but inside the place was quite neat. The furniture was old, but at least it wasn't one of those old people's places that was stuffed to the ceiling with all kinds of pictures and little doo-dads. Willard seemed to have only the necessities, and they were all sort of orderly. But the house smelled lousy—like a greasy truck stop.

Willard kept right on going through the living room and kitchen, and then he opened a door and flipped on a light over some stairs. "It's down here," he said, and started down the steps to the basement.

"Hey, you're not some kind of weirdo, are you?" Mark said.

Willard laughed, harder than he had before, but that set him off coughing. He had to stop on the stairs for a moment until the coughing subsided and he could get his breath. "I'm weird, all right," he finally said. "You'll see what I'm talking about in just a minute."

Willard slowly walked down the last steps, and then he fumbled around to find the light switch. Mark waited, wondering what to expect, but then the light came on and Willard stepped aside so that Mark could come the rest of the way into the old basement. It took Mark a moment to realize what he was looking at. Half the basement was taken up with a huge layout for electric trains—except that there were no trains and the old board was filthy dirty. Mark walked over to it. The center of the layout dropped into a big canyon, but Mark could see when he got closer that this was the control center. There were three electrical panels inside. Mountains ranged all the way around the canyon, except at the front it was flat, and it was there that the railroad station and yard were located. There were three main tracks that looped around the board, through tunnels and across bridges, but in the yard there must have been ten lines, and there was a large red roundhouse with a turntable in front of it. A little town stood in the back, off in the mountains. It seemed to be a mining town, built in against the side of a hill.

"Did you make this?" Mark asked.

"Yup."

"It's big."

Willard chuckled, his breath coming in jerks. "It's big all right. I worked on it for years."

"How come you don't use it anymore?"

"I don't know. I had one before that I built when my kids were home—it was a big O-guage layout—but when we moved into this house, back in 1961, I didn't have much room down here, so I decided to build one with H-O stuff—that's the smaller trains. Back then not so many worked with the little ones, but now it's about all you see. When I first retired I worked on it a lot, and I had it in pretty good shape, but I just let it go later on—lost interest in it, I guess."

"So what are you going to do with it now?"

"Well, that's what I been thinking about. I'm thinking I might fix it up. I'd like to get some new trains. They sure make some nice ones these days. I need to tear off a lot of that old grass and put down that new stuff. And I need to fix up some of them hills that are falling in."

"It's going to take a lot of work, isn't it?"

"Yuh, sure. But it's something to do."

Mark looked at all the detail, the little hobo figures sitting under a bridge and the little cars and trucks in the mining town. He wondered why anyone would want to spend so much time on a big toy.

"But I need someone to help me. I can't get back under the board very well anymore. To work in the back I have to go under and come up behind them mountains. I got places that open up back there. I need someone young who can get into them. Do you think you might be interested?"

Mark looked at the board, not at Willard. "No," he said, "I don't think so."

"Oh." Mark glanced up. Willard was squinting and his bushy white eyebrows were pulled tight over his eyes. He coughed again, a loose, rough cough. "Well, all right. I'd be willing to pay you something—you know—if you wanted to come over once in a while after school and just do some of the things I can't do anymore."

The last thing he needed, Mark thought, was to get tied up with this old guy. He had never played much with electric trains when he was a kid, and he was not really interested in starting now that he was thirteen years old. But the money was sort of tempting. He never had enough to play Space Invaders at the arcade. "No, I don't think so," he said, however. "There must be some other guys around here who would do it."

"That's a laugh," Willard said. Mark looked over at him, wondering what he meant. "The boys around this neighborhood don't care about nothing like that. You're the only one who doesn't smart off to me and call me gramps."

"They're a bunch of jerks," Mark said.

"Well, I wasn't no angel when I was a kid," Willard said. "But anyway, I could pay you a little something if you could just stop by once in a while and help me out. I'm going to go down and buy some things tomorrow. I might even start taking up some of this track tonight."

"What's wrong with the track?"

"Well, I used a lot of that snap-together stuff last time. But now I want to do it right. I'm going to lay it by hand this time."

"What do you mean?"

"I'm going to lay each tie, one at a time, and then put down longer runs of track, without so many breaks in 'em."

Mark thought that was really stupid. He couldn't imagine a more tedious job. "Well, I don't think so," he finally said, but he couldn't stand to look at the old man when he said it.

"Well, all right. But stop by some time, okay? At least have a look at what I'm doing. And then if you could help me even clean it off once, especially back in the back, I'd appreciate it."

"Okay. I guess I could do something like that." But Mark knew he really had no intention of coming back again.

"Good. Come tomorrow afternoon if you can—or just whenever you get a chance."

Willard actually sounded a little excited. He began to cough again, and Mark sort of felt sorry for him. But who needed to hang around with some old guy like that? The man had to be eighty years old.

CHAPTER 2

~~~~~~

School the next day was pretty much the usual routine. In math, Mrs. Pederson gave him a bad time about not finishing his homework. But Mark had learned that he was better off when he kept his mouth shut and didn't give any excuses. Then she was soon left with nothing to say. He did finally commit himself to getting caught up, but when he left the school that afternoon he didn't even take his math book with him. He took it out of his locker and then slammed it back in. And he hurried to get on the bus early, so that he could get a seat on the opposite side from the day before. He didn't want to be sitting where Willard could see him.

Whittington and Anders did their usual bit, yelling their insults at "gramps," even though Willard was nowhere in sight and they had to shout their comments at the house itself. Obviously they were content with the laughter they got from the kids, whether Willard actually heard or not. In some ways, Mark found Anders more disgusting than Whittington. He was a grimy kid with decaying teeth and stringy hair, and he had a really filthy mouth. He loved to use vile words in front of girls and watch for their reactions. As usual, Mark was just glad to get off the bus.

He walked down the street wondering what to do. He still didn't want to admit to himself that he was going over to Willard's. But all day it had been on his mind. The worst thing of all was to have nothing to do. That's when his troubles always started—and the words came back to him. The best thing was playing Space Invaders at the arcade. When he was playing, he could forget everything else. But for that he needed money. He had long since shot his allowance. If he could hang around Willard's long enough to pick up a little cash, then he could head down to the arcade before his mother got home.

Ronnie, Mark's little brother, never got home as early as Mark did, but Mark was supposed to keep an eye on him until Mom got home. But Mark figured that Ronnie would be outside playing anyway and that if he took off for a little while, it wouldn't really hurt anything.

When Mark knocked on Willard's door, he looked around to make sure no one saw him. He had to knock three times before Willard finally showed up. "Ah, Austin, good," Willard said, but he was out of breath. "I'm sorry I took so long. I was downstairs. When you come again, just walk in."

"Don't you lock your door?"

"Oh, no. I never have. I ain't going to start now."

Mark walked downstairs, following Willard. The smell of dampness—and rot—in the stairway bothered Mark. He didn't really want to go down into this old place with the old man. This would be the only time.

"I'll tell you what, Austin. You go underneath and come up through that opening behind those hills in the corner." He pointed to the spot. The opening could not be seen from the front of the board. "Take this rag and try to dust off what you can, especially the cobwebs. And just pull those trees right off. There's a new kind that you can buy kits for. They look a lot better. I might end up putting a new layer of plaster over those hills, and then paint 'em again, but for now let's at least clean 'em up." Mark crouched down to go under the front of the board. "Oh, Austin, take this screwdriver back too. If you don't mind, you could take off some of that track back there."

Mark could see that Willard was getting him more involved than he wanted to be, but he took the screwdriver and the rag and made his way to the opening. He stood up and took a look around.

"Can you see what needs cleaning back there, Austin?"

"Sure." He jabbed at a cobweb with the rag. "My name's Mark," he said.

"Oh, all right. I guess I got used to always calling people by their last names when I was with the railroad. We always done that. I ain't been called anything but Willard for thirty or forty years, I guess."

"Is that your last name, then?"

"Oh, yes. But it's my first name, too. You don't need to call me Mister or nothing like that—just Willard. That's all anybody calls me." Willard straightened up for a moment and rubbed one of his hands along the small of his back. He had on the same old overalls he had worn the day before. "Come to think of it, I guess nobody calls me anything anymore. Except those kids that call me gramps."

Mark tried to get the dust off the hills around him, but the rough texture made it hard. Still, he got the corner looking a little better, and then he started taking up track. Willard was working along the front edge of the board, where the main yard was, with row after row of tracks. Mark wondered how long he would have to hang around before Willard would pay him something. Would he pay today, or would there be a payday later? What he wanted was a buck or two and enough time to get to the arcade for a while.

"Did you work for the railroad a long time?" Mark asked, but he didn't know why. He didn't really care.

"Sure did. Thirty-five years."

"I guess you must have gone all over the place then?"

"Well, yes and no. When I actually worked for the railroad, I didn't go nowhere. I stayed right in the yard. I was a switchman, and then later I worked on the big locomotives, keeping them serviced and oiled."

"Was that here in Denver?"

"For a long time it was. But I didn't come to Colorado until just before the war broke out. Before that I was in Kansas City, and before that, Omaha. And before that, all over the place.

"What do you mean?"

"Oh, well, I could tell you some real stories, Austin. I was full of hell when I was a young fellow. I had more jobs and lost 'em than I could ever count. I worked at all sorts of things before I settled into railroad work. I guess I figured I owed 'em something, since I'd taken so many free rides." He laughed in his usual way, his head bobbing and his lips slipping back over his worn-out teeth. He seemed to be sucking in air when he laughed, as though the effort strained him.

"Did you hitch trains?" Mark asked. He looked up from his work. Old Willard was grinning still, and a shock of white hair had fallen across his forehead— like a little boy's.

"I sure did. I been everywhere, Austin. There ain't

no place in this country I ain't seen—not if a train goes to it."

"It sounds like fun," Mark said. And it did. It sounded absolutely wonderful. There was nothing Mark wanted more than freedom—everyone off his back, and just time to wander.

"Oh, it was fun all right. But it was stupid, too. I never had a brain in my head in them days. I was always getting myself drunk and doing something crazy. I ended up in jail a couple of times."

"What for?"

"Fighting." Willard was grinning again. "I was a real fighter, too. I was big in those days, and strong. I remember one time I broke a man's collarbone right in half."

"His collarbone?"

"Yuh. I took a swing at him and meant to hit him in the head, but I guess he stepped into it or something, and I hit the man right in the shoulder—in here by the neck—and I heard that bone snap right off. I never seen a man turn so white."

Mark was having a little trouble picturing old Willard that way. And he was embarrassed when Willard just kept looking at him, grinning and nodding. Mark went back to work.

"But it was stupid," Willard said. "I never built up nothing. It was Depression years and most men was trying to hang on to what they could, but not me. I spent everything I had on drinking and womanizing and gambling—everything that don't last."

"I thought you said you were married?"

"Well, I was. But not till I went to Kansas City. That's when I first started to settle down some. And I guess I still didn't make things easy for that poor woman. At least not for a while."

"Did she die?"

"Yup. But we was married thirty-four years, almost thirty-five. She just died about three years ago. I wasn't ready for that though. She was quite a little bit younger than me, and I always figured I'd go first."

Mark decided he wasn't going to push the conversation any further. He didn't want Willard to start thinking that he was really all that interested.

Willard straightened his back again, and then he brushed the hair out of his eyes. His old hands were brown and used up, the fingers bent in on each other, and the knuckles knobbed out of shape. "If I was doing it over again, though, I guess I'd do some things differ'nt. I don't suppose I'd go to college or anything like that—never had the brains for it—but I'd save my money a little better when I was young, not just waste it all." He stopped and grunted at a screw that wouldn't come loose. "But I have to admit, I did have me a good time back in those days. I guess that's worth something. Now that I'm here by myself, at least it's something to look back on and laugh about."

"What happened to your kids? Didn't you say you had some?"

"I guess I do—though you wouldn't know it. I've got a daughter and three sons. My daughter calls me once in a while. She lives in California. And one of my boys writes once or twice a year, or at least his wife does. But the other two, they're about like I was. They're both wilder than March hares. I think the one is in Texas, and I don't have any idea about the other one. He's probably in jail somewhere."

Mark had removed all the track he could reach from where he was, but he could see another opening a little way down the board. A section of the mountain had to be lifted off to get through it. Mark knelt down and then worked his way over to the opening and pushed up the lift-off section. When he came up Willard said, "That's the idea. You're getting this thing figured out already. I'll bet you're a good student, huh?"

"No. I'm not," Mark said, but he was not going to talk about that. He didn't want any speeches about "buckling down." "So, did you like working on the railroad?" he asked, trying to push the conversation back at Willard.

"Well, it was a job, and a pretty good one for a long time. Back during the war, and for a while after, everybody took the trains. They were snazzy outfits in those days, and train stations was beautiful places. They weren't all rundown like they are now. I used to get passes, and me and the wife would go down to California or back east somewheres. We had some mighty nice trips." Willard had taken up a lot of track and had stacked it in neat piles along the front of the board. Mark tried to do the same.

"Some of the people I worked with got on my nerves after so many years," Willard said, and his voice was gradually growing softer, even distant, as though he were talking to himself more than to Mark. "But I had some awful good friends, too. Most of 'em are dead now. I worked with two fellows almost all the years I was down there. And then after we all retired, we used to go to this one park not too far from here, and we used to play pinochle with some other men, or just sit around and kill some time together. Both of them are dead now though—one died just last year. I guess everybody I know is dead or about to get that way."

Mark didn't really want to hear any more of this. He was starting to get nervous. Soon he'd have to get some money out of old Willard and get out of here. Best to stay a while longer though. He wasn't likely to get much if he left before an hour was even up.

Willard picked up a stack of tracks, took them over to a corner of the basement and set them down near the concrete wall. When he stood up, he took a long, wheezy breath and began to cough. "Oh, boy," he said, after a moment, "I can't bend very easy anymore. It about breaks me in half." He stood straight, putting both hands against the small of his back. "Ol' McGill —he was one of my friends—he used to say, 'I wouldn't mind my body quitting on me so much, if my memory would just go out on me, too. Then I wouldn't know what I was missing.'"

Willard laughed, and then he went back to the

board and picked up his screwdriver. "McGill, he was some fellow. And so was ol' Gurney. Those two never stopped. I guess all three of us never did. But Gurney was the only guy I ever knew who could keep up with McGill, and he was always egging him into something or another." Willard was chuckling to himself, looking down at the track. For some reason it made Mark feel self-conscious and a little sad. But he really didn't need anything like this, he really didn't.

"See, McGill had a whole bunch of kids. I guess it was seven or eight of 'em. And Gurney was always teasing him about his wife having babies all the time. Gurney would say, 'Morning, McGill. Did your wife have another baby last night?' That's how he talked, with a big, deep voice like that. And ol' McGill he was just the opposite. His voice was sort of high, even though he was a heck of a big man. He'd come right back. 'Yuh,' he'd say, 'She had twins. But they're sure a couple of hard-lookers, them two. When I first seen 'em they didn't have no diapers on, and I couldn't tell one end of 'em from the other.' "

Willard chuckled to himself again. Mark thought ol' Gurney and McGill sounded pretty stupid. How long was he going to have to hang around? He moved down to the opening in the far corner and tried to clean up the worst of the dirt that was on the hills around the little mining town, deciding to wait for another ten minutes.

Willard went on with his stories about his friends, until finally Mark said, "Well, Mr.—or Willard—I better take off now. My mom will be getting home pretty soon."

"All right. That's fine. Now let me see. You stayed about an hour. What if I paid you a dollar? Is that enough? I know that ain't a lot, but. . . ."

"That's fine, Willard." Mark was crawling out from under the board. When he stood up, Willard had his wallet out, and he handed Mark a dollar.

"There yuh go, Austin. I hope it's enough. I would sure like to have you come back again and. . . ."

"Yuh, I'll come over again sometime." But Mark knew he wouldn't.

"Good. I can get most of the rest of the track off, and then—oh, I didn't show you the train I bought, did I?" He turned and walked to the bench at the far end of the basement. When he got there, he lifted the top off a big flat box and then stepped aside so that Mark could see. There was a silver locomotive with red stripes, a Santa Fe, and seven or eight freight cars. "She's a beauty, ain't she?" Willard said.

"Yuh, it's pretty nice," Mark said, immediately embarrassed by his obvious lack of interest.

Willard said nothing for a time, and then he put the lid back on the box. "Listen, Austin," he said. "I didn't mean to get so carried away with my old memories. I know you don't want to hear all my stories about McGill and that sort of—" He stopped for a moment as though he couldn't think of what to say. "What I mean is, if you come back, I won't start into that again, all right?"

"That was all right, Willard. It didn't bother me." Mark was lying, and he suspected they both knew it. He could feel the tension in his voice.

"Well, it's easy for an old man to start in that way. I guess that's why young people don't—"

"No, it was all right, Willard. Really. Those guys must have been pretty funny." It was a lame thing to say, stupid and lame.

Willard looked at him for a moment, his eyes squinting a little. "Yuh, they was funny," he finally said, but the sadness in his voice caused Mark to look away.

"I knew a guy kind of like them," Mark said. "He used to always say, 'If you think I'm ugly, you ought to see my brother. At least I got one eye on each side of my nose.' "

Willard didn't laugh. Mark didn't either. It was an uncomfortable moment. "Well, come over tomorrow if you feel like it."

Mark said he would and thought maybe he meant it; but he hurried down to the arcade. If he got back late for dinner, his mother would be mad; but if he didn't go before she got home, he might not get to go at all.

CHAPTER 3

▬▬▬▬▬▬▬▬▬▬▬▬▬▬▬▬▬▬▬▬▬▬▬▬

When Mark got home his mother and Ronnie were already eating. "Where have you been?" she asked.

Mark sat down at the table without saying anything. His mother had cooked some of that quickie macaroni and cheese that comes out of a box, and she had heated up some canned peas. Mark hated that kind of macaroni, and canned peas made him gag. But he slopped some of each on his plate. Mom was already upset. All he needed to do was complain about the food.

"I said, where have you been?"

"Just knocking around."

"He's been down at the arcade, I'll bet," Ronnie said.

"Shut your mouth, you little creep. You don't know where I've been."

"I saw you walking that way." Ronnie was in third grade, but like Mark, he was small for his age. Mark thought he acted like a baby—and that Mom treated him that way. He was a plump little kid who was always claiming he was sick when anything needed to be done around the house. He had always been sort of slow in school, and he had been in the hospital a couple of times because of some sort of kidney infection. Maybe that's why Mom always seemed to give him special care, but Mark thought the kid would be better off if she kicked his behind once in a while.

"Mark, *were* you at the arcade?"

"Yes."

"Where did you get the money?"

"Who said I had any money? I didn't say I played any of the games."

"Well, did you?" His mother looked tired. She was only thirty-three. Most people considered her a real beauty, but for some reason it embarrassed Mark that she wore so much makeup and always had her hair bleached so blonde. She didn't look like a mother— she looked more like a movie star—except she wasn't *that* pretty. In fact, by this time of day she looked sort of worn-out and droopy. She worked as a receptionist in the front office of a big company that made missile parts and munitions. More than anything else, she answered the phone. Because she didn't have any secretarial training, she didn't get paid very much.

"*Well*, did you?"

"Yes. I played a couple of times."

"All right, Mark. Let's lay off this twenty-questions stuff. I'm too tired for that. Where did you get the money?"

"I worked for it, all right? I earned a lousy dollar for working for an hour, and I went to the arcade and spent every penny of it in *one* place. All right?"

Ronnie said, "You don't have to start yelling."

"Shut up, Ronnie, or I'll push your fat little face in. Do you hear me?"

"*Mark*." His mother looked more frustrated than angry. Her eyes seemed tired. Under the makeup, lines were beginning to form, crow's feet that were spreading out from the corners of her eyes. Something about his mother depressed Mark. She looked defeated. But he did shut his mouth, then took his plate to the sink and washed most of the food off and headed for his room. "Mark, wait. Come back and sit down for a minute. I want to talk to you."

Mark turned around, but he didn't go back. "What?" he said.

"Mark, I'm not trying to give you the third degree. I just worry about you. There are so many things happening to kids your age these days. I need to know where you're going and what you're doing—and I'm not here in the afternoons, so I get worried when—"

"You don't have to worry, all right?" His voice was full of sarcasm. "I don't smoke pot; I don't drop pills; I don't even drink beer. I—"

"I tasted a beer once," Ronnie said. "Dad let me.—"

"Ronnie, not right now, okay?" Mother said.

"I've never gone out with a girl in my life—so you don't need to worry about that. And I don't—"

"Okay, Mark. Okay." She put her hand to her forehead and leaned forward, letting her long hair fall down across her face. Mark was sort of sorry he had come on so strong, but he didn't know how to take any of it back.

"Can I go now?"

"Why don't you help me with the dishes, Mark?" She looked up at him. "I would just like to talk to you for a few minutes." She stood up. The knit dress she was wearing—light blue—clung to her and showed what a nice figure she had. Mark leaned against the cabinets and stared at the worn-out linoleum on the floor. He didn't want to help with the dishes. "Ronnie, why don't you run outside for a while, and Mark and I will do the dishes, okay?"

"I want to watch television."

"All right. Do that. But don't turn it up too loud, okay?"

The living room—where the television set was—was just off the kitchen. Mark knew that Ronnie wanted to listen to the conversation. But if Mom had asked him to watch TV, he would have said he wanted to go outside.

Mrs. Austin put on an apron and filled the sink with hot water. One of the things she often said she would like to have was a dishwasher, but she couldn't afford one. They had had one in their bigger house— the one they had lived in when Dad had still been alive. But they hadn't gotten much insurance money, and now they had to survive on what Mom could earn.

"I'm glad to hear you worked today, Mark. Where did you work?"

"Mom, do we have to get into all that? I just helped an old guy out for a while this afternoon, and he gave me a buck. Okay?"

His mother put both her hands on the edge of the cabinet and looked down for several seconds. "Mark," she said, "what's wrong? I can't say *anything* to you. You talk to me like you hate me."

Mark took a deep breath. He didn't want to go through this again tonight. "I don't hate you, Mom," he said, but there was no gentleness in his voice.

"Why do you talk to me that way?"

"What way?"

"You know what I mean, Mark. You're always hostile with me—no matter what I say."

"You talk the same way to me."

She straightened up, and then for a time she looked out the window that was in front of the sink. Mark had picked up a dish towel, but he was just standing back from his mother, waiting. It was getting dark outside, dreary-looking, faded.

"I know that's true sometimes, Mark. But I get so frustrated. You won't let me talk to you—and so I get angry. Ever since your dad died, you've—"

"Mom, I don't want to talk about that again. I don't see any point in it."

"But you have to talk about it. It's pretty obvious that it's bothering you. You've quit studying in school. You won't make friends. You talk to me like I'm your enemy. You scream at Ronnie no matter what he says." Mark glanced at Ronnie and could see that he was listening to every word, hardly even looking at the television set. "Mark, the only thing you want to do is play that space game at the arcade. It's just not normal to care about nothing at all except playing a silly game."

Mark didn't answer. They had gone through this conversation ten times before—twenty times. His mother took a long breath and let it out slowly; then she turned around, facing him. "Honey, I know it's been hard for you. I know you loved him in spite of the way he sometimes treated you. I know it wasn't easy the *way* he died. But you can't keep it all inside and just—"

"Listen, Mom. I'm going to tell you this for the last time. And then I don't ever want to talk about it again. I *hated* him. And I still do. He never did one thing to make me feel any other way. I don't care that he's dead. I didn't care on the day that he died—and you didn't see me crying at his funeral. And I don't care now." Mark said the words, but his voice was tense, full of emotion, and even he knew there was more to the whole thing than he was admitting. But he did not want to *talk* about it.

"Then why have you changed so much, Mark? Since he died you've been different. You have to admit that."

Mark stood, holding the dish towel in both hands, looking down. "No, I don't," he said, but his voice was changed, more subdued. "I don't like this school. I don't have any friends over there."

"But you need to try, honey. You aren't trying at all. Remember when we moved into the other neighborhood—when you were just little? You knew every kid in the area within a couple of days. That's how you always used to be. You were a lot like your dad in that way."

Mark didn't say anything. He wanted her to quit. It didn't do any good to answer, he should have remembered that; it only got her started again. She waited for a time and then turned around to put some of the dishes in the water. Mark started bringing those that were still on the table over to the sink. For several minutes nothing more was said. Mark began to wipe off the dishes that his mother placed in the drying rack.

"Mark, there's something else I want to talk to you about."

He waited, continuing to dry the plate he was holding, but he didn't say anything.

"Don is coming over Friday evening." Mark stopped. He held the plate and the towel, but he didn't move at all. "He wants to take you and Ronnie with us. He thought maybe we could drive up into the mountains or something—maybe have a picnic."

Mark said nothing for a time, but he began to wipe the plate again. It was long since dry. "I have a thing at school I have to go to that night," he said.

"Mark, I'm sorry, but I don't think that's true. You haven't gone to anything at this school since you got here."

"All right, then, call me a liar." The heat was back in his voice. And part of the reason was that she was right—he *was* lying.

"No, Mark, I don't want to call you a liar, but you'll have to admit that—"

"I don't admit to anything. I have a play I'm supposed to go to. My English teacher said we *have* to go."

"What play?"

"Come on, Mom, lay off. I don't know what play. I don't care either."

"Mark, it's Don, isn't it? You don't like him."

"I don't even know the guy. I've only seen him a few times when he's been here to get you."

"He's really very nice, Mark. He's so different from . . . from what we've experienced before. And he has a good job and is really the kind of guy I've always wanted to get to know." She reached up and pushed some strands of hair back over her shoulder.

"Great, Mom. What do I care? But I have to go to the play."

"All right. Maybe we can go on Sunday afternoon. I'll ask him about it. I *know* you don't have anything that day. Why don't we plan on it? I want you to get to know him, honey. He was quite an athlete in school; he could help you with your basketball."

"Okay, Mom. I'll go on the picnic." But he threw down the dish towel and went to his room.

In his bedroom he flipped on the radio, but the disc jockey was talking, and Mark turned it back off. He wished he had a stereo. Maybe dear old Don would buy him a stereo if he married Mother. But the thought was overwhelming. He grabbed his pillow and punched it, picked it up and punched it again. Too bad he'd spent all his money at the arcade. He wanted to go back. He wanted to play Space Invaders. If he stayed in his room alone, doing nothing, the words would all come back again. He couldn't face that tonight.

CHAPTER 4

When Friday came, Mark carried out his act. He told his mother he was going to the play. She wanted to know why he didn't dress up a little better, but Mark said he didn't think it was necessary and took off. He suspected that she still didn't believe him, but as long as she didn't press him, he didn't much care.

What Mark needed was money. His mother always gave him an allowance at the first of the month—five dollars. But he usually shot that the first week. For a while he had tried skipping lunch and using his lunch money to play Space Invaders, but his mother had found out and had demanded that he eat every day. He still did it once in a while, but she was always asking him if he had eaten and what had been served. Mark really didn't like lying—even though he did it sometimes—and so he had given in and started having lunch most of the time.

The only way he knew to pick up any money tonight was to go back to Willard's place. He thought that if he could hang around Willard's for an hour or so, maybe he could get another dollar, and then he could head for the arcade. He hated to go back, and he hadn't really planned to, but he couldn't think of any other options.

Mark knocked on Willard's door, even though the old guy had told him to walk right in. When no one answered, however, he opened the door. "Hey, Willard, you here?" He didn't hear anything, so he stepped inside and shut the door behind him, then walked through the living room to the kitchen. The door to the basement was open, and the light over the stairs was on. "Hey, Willard, you down there?"

"Sure. Come on down. Is that you, Austin?"

"Mark." He started down the stairs, but already he regretted coming. What a lousy way to shoot his time on a Friday evening.

"Say, how yuh doing?" Willard said, as Mark stepped into the room. "I was starting to think you weren't coming back."

"Well, I've been kind of busy."

"What did you do, go out for basketball?" Willard asked, grinning with all his old stained teeth.

Mark tried to sound serious. "Yuh. I'm the third baseman."

Willard had turned toward the train layout. He was about to say something else when his head popped around. "Third base? On a basketball team?"

"That's just what the coach keeps saying," Mark said, still looking as serious as he could.

"You know something, Austin? You're one strange kid. You're going to turn into a very weird old man some day." Willard was trying to look serious too, but he couldn't do it.

Mark was sort of sorry he had goofed around with the old guy. He hated to let Willard think he was going to be his buddy, or something of that sort. "Looks like you've done a lot of work," Mark said.

"Well, yuh. I'm glad to know it looks like it. I sure got a lot ahead of me." Mark walked over to the board. Willard had been working mainly up front, it appeared; he had taken up all the old track in the yard, and he had begun the slow task of laying the individual ties for the new rails.

"Do you have to glue each one of those little ties?"

"Ain't no other way."

"Is it really that much better than the track you just snap together?"

Willard looked toward Mark, squinting, his eyebrows hanging over his eyes. "Well, I don't know,

Austin. Now that I'm getting into it, I wonder myself. But it will make a smoother run for the trains—and then—well, I guess I'm getting some strange notions in my old age."

"What do you mean?"

"I want this to be as much like the real thing as I can make it. I'm going to take out that whole little mining town, and I'm going to do it all over again. If I have the time, I might even hand-build all the new places. I done that on the roundhouse, and on that old coal loader, you know."

"But can't you buy that kind of stuff?"

"Sure you can. But that's what I done last time, and I never did feel like it was just right. See, most of this stuff would have been used, about like it is, in the forties and even in the early fifties. But that old town is more like you would have seen clear back in the twenties, or maybe even earlier. It just don't look right."

So who cared? Mark couldn't believe the old guy. Probably no one in the world would ever come down in this old basement to look at the thing, and here he was worrying about whether it *looked* just right. "When are you going to have enough track on so that you can run some trains?"

"Actually, we could do that tonight, if you helped me with that one section back beyond those hills. See, I'm not going to take all of that track up. What's in the tunnels and on the bridges I'm just going to have to leave—at least for now. But if you could lay the new ties back on that one straight run, I could finish up this section, and we could put the new train on."

Willard actually sounded excited. Mark was embarrassed for him. But he crawled under the board and went back to the opening near the track that Willard wanted him to work on. He figured out what he would need, and then he went back for the ties and glue. He watched Willard for a time and asked a few questions before he actually tried to do any himself, but when he did, he found the process a little less difficult than he had expected. It took time, however. The board had to be scraped clean so that everything was level, and then each tie had to be set precisely, lined up and parallel. Mark found himself totally absorbed in the work before long, and time went by much faster than he had expected.

Eventually Willard had to bend down and struggle his way under the board to the center opening so that he could look at what Mark had done. He came up puffing, and he had to stop and straighten his back for a time. But when he saw Mark's work, he said, "Say, Austin, you've done real fine there. You catch on to things fast, don't you?"

"I don't know."

"Well, you sure do. Do you take a shop class over at school?"

"Yuh."

"What've you been making?"

"A stupid shelf. The shop teacher makes you sand it until your arm falls off."

"But that's what it takes, Austin. With woodwork you have to do a lot of sanding to make it look right." But then he looked up from the track. "You know, you're just the way I was at your age. You don't like doing anything that some grown-up tells you that you have to do. Right?"

"I don't know." Mark didn't think that was true, but he had never really thought about it. And he didn't want to. If Willard would just mind his own business, he wouldn't be so bad.

By the time they had the track on, completing the large loop, more than two hours had gone by, but Mark hadn't thought much about it. He was sort of curious to see the train take a run. Willard brought the box over, and the two of them took out the new train. Willard set out the engine, making sure that the wheels were set correctly on the track. "Austin," he said, "could you set the rest of those cars out. I've been bending over too much tonight. My back is just about broke." He strained to push his shoulders back, and he took a deep breath, but that only set him off coughing. Mark put the rest of the cars out. He had never owned an electric train, but some of his friends had, and he had played with them enough to know how the wheels had to be lined up.

The little train was amazingly realistic. There were a couple of regular box cars, but there was also a tanker and a flat car loaded with logs, and there was even one with a little crane on it. When Mark put down the caboose and got it coupled with the others, he said, "All right, Willard, let's let it rip."

"Now wait a minute. You get under, in the middle there and go ahead and start 'er out, but we don't want to 'let it rip.' In the first place, we gotta make sure the track is right; but even without that, it ain't the way you do it. It takes a lot of power to get a train going. They don't just take off out of the yard like a race car."

What was he talking about? This thing wasn't a real train. Mark wondered if the old man was getting senile. But he didn't say anything. What difference did it make? He figured he had at least two bucks coming, and he wanted to get down to the arcade before it got much later.

Willard told him which lever to push down, and when he did, the light on the engine came on, and the little train slowly chugged out of the yard. It made a sound that was surprisingly realistic. Willard told him to give it a little more power, but it never did go very fast. It worked its way into the hills, through a tunnel, around past the mining town, and then across the hills in the back and the bridge over a deep ravine. It swung slowly behind the roundhouse, through another tunnel, and finally back into the yard.

"Well, we done all right," Willard said. "There's a click where it comes out of the first tunnel, but we could just about expect that."

"Can I give it a little more power?" Mark asked.

"Just a little."

Mark kicked up the speed a fair amount, however, and he actually found himself rather involved in watching the train make its loop again. "When we get the other lines in, where else can we run it to?"

"Well, see those switches, out there by the tunnels?"

"Yuh."

"It'll take that higher loop out there in those hills, if you switch into it. And we can switch it out of the yard, too, directly into the mining town."

"What about the line up above, in the back?"

"It won't go up there. That's strictly for the old locomotive that runs to the mine and back. The main line doesn't switch into it."

"How many trains could we have going at once?"

"Well, three, if we was careful. But we'll have us a lot of trains here in the yard, and a bunch of engines for the roundhouse. Then we can switch back and forth, make up the trains we want to, and head 'em out on the main track."

"Does that turntable really work?"

"It doesn't now. There's a wire loose or something, but we'll get it going. We'll have ourselves a real layout here in a few months."

A few months? Mark stepped back a little, away from the control panels. He was getting himself into something really stupid. He looked over at Willard who was still watching the train intently, his thumbs tucked under the shoulder straps of his overalls. "She's a beauty, ain't she?" he said.

Mark didn't answer. Now he just wanted to get his money and get out of there. So he let the train swing around into the yard again, and he slowly shut down the power. Then he crawled under the board and came out to where Willard was standing.

"Ain't I an old fool?" the man said. "Playing with choo-choo trains." He put his hand on Mark's shoulder.

Mark stepped a little further away, and Willard dropped his hand. It was time to go, and there had to be a smooth way of getting out, without actually mentioning the money. But Willard began to explain the switching system, and it wasn't long—in spite of his promise of the time before—until he was reminiscing about his old days as a switchman. Mark just let him talk for a while, and eventually, to be polite, he said, "I guess it's quite a responsibility."

"Switching? Oh, yuh, I guess it is. But any ol' fool can do it. Even me. Even ol' Gurney and McGill could do it, and neither one of them had the brains of a gnat." Willard laughed to himself, quietly, nodding his head.

"Were they really that dumb?"

Willard grinned, and then he sucked at the back of his teeth, making a little smacking sound. "Oh, shoot, I don't know. No, I guess they weren't dumb—not either one of 'em—but they was sure crazy."

Mark pulled his hand out of his jeans' pocket and

tried to roll his wrist around enough to see his watch. He really had to get out of there before it got much later. "I remember one time," Willard said, "ol' McGill come into work, and he was pulling on his work overalls. Ol' Gurney comes up to him and says, 'I guess your wife is expecting again by now, ain't she?' " Willard had dropped his jaw and held his chin down, as he tried to make his voice as deep as possible; but now in a much higher voice, he said, " 'Well, of course. We ain't had a new baby for a week.' And so then Gurney says, 'And how's the little one doing?' McGill, he looked up, sort of like he was worried, and he says, 'Well, he ain't too bad, but he sure does have a mean streak in him. A couple of nights ago he up and grabbed our little dog and ate him.' 'He ate yer dog?' Gurney says, just like he was serious as can be. 'He sure did,' McGill says, and then Gurney, he says, 'That's terrible.' But ol' McGill just sort of shook his head, and then he says, 'Yuh, it shore was, but it ain't the dog I felt so bad about.' 'What do you mean it ain't the dog?' Gurney says. 'Well,' McGill says, 'I guess I can get me a new dog—he was given to me anyhow. But I sure hated to lose that nice new collar and chain.' "

Willard laughed again, his breath coming in bursts. Mark laughed a little too, but it took some effort. "But here I go again," Willard said, "starting in on my old stories. All I can say is that you gotta be a stupid kid to laugh at something like that." He put his hand on Mark's shoulder again.

"Well, I could be worse," Mark said.

"How's that?"

"I could be the old guy who forced some stupid kid to listen to a dumb story like that."

Willard laughed for some time. "You're all right, Austin," he said. "You're some kid."

Mark finally got his money—two and a half dollars —and he headed down to the arcade immediately. By the time he got home it was after midnight. He knew his mother wouldn't like it, but he didn't much care. At least he had had a whole evening of peace.

CHAPTER 5

‖‖‖‖‖‖‖‖‖‖‖‖‖‖‖‖‖‖‖‖‖‖‖‖‖‖‖‖‖‖‖‖‖‖‖‖‖‖‖

Sunday morning—or actually it was noon by the time they got away—the Austins went on their picnic with Don. All the way up the highway into the mountains, Don and Mrs. Austin chatted about this and that, and Ronnie occasionally had something to say, but Mark sat in the back seat and said nothing. It was a big, roomy car, an old Pontiac, and Don had obviously taken good care of it. It looked as though no one had ever been in the back seat before. It was not at all like Mark's dad's old car, which had always been full of empty pop bottles and candy bar wrappers.

"Mark," Don said, looking back over his shoulder, "how's school going these days?"

"Okay, I guess," Mark said, hardly loudly enough to be heard.

"Do you like your new school?"

"Not really."

"Why not?"

"I don't know. I just don't."

"Yuh, well, it's always hard to make a switch like that. You'll get used to it." Mark didn't say anything. He hoped Don wouldn't push the conversation. There was something about the guy that really bugged Mark. He was just so darn *nice*. But underneath it all, Mark wondered if it wasn't all an act. Mom had said that Don had been married once before and had a couple of kids. Maybe he hadn't been so *sweet* to his wife and kids as he pretended to be now.

"Are you going out for any of the teams this year, Mark?" Don asked.

"No."

"Why not?"

"I'm no good."

"Your mother tells me you shoot at that old basketball hoop a lot. How would it be if I came over and we set up a new basket—so it was regulation height—and then I helped you with your shooting and ball handling? I used to be pretty good, back when I was in high school."

Mark didn't even want to answer, but Don waited

and the silence became awkward. "No, that's all right," Mark finally said.

"I'd be happy to do it. How would it be if I came over some night this week?"

"No. You'd just be wasting your time."

Mark could see Don's eyes in the rearview mirror. He was looking through the mirror at Mark, and he was anxious, his voice a little strained. In a way Mark felt sorry for him because he was trying so hard, but the last thing Mark wanted was to be out in back playing basketball with him every night. He would probably show up in one of his knit shirts, and with a pair of Adidas on—and a whistle around his neck. And he would want to be so *helpful*. He was trying to be Mark's father—that's what he was up to.

"It's something I would enjoy, Mark. I need the exercise myself. How about tomorrow, or maybe Tuesday?"

"No, thanks. I'd rather not." Mark saw his mother's neck straighten and her shoulders pull back. The silence that followed was terribly uncomfortable. Don said nothing for a while, then finally reached over and turned the radio on. It was on one of those FM "easy listening" stations. Mark hated that kind of music. It would take someone like Don to listen to junk like that.

After a few minutes Don and his mother went back to their own small talk, but they seemed self-conscious and a little awkward. Mark was embarrassed, partly for himself and partly for them. But it was easier to live with that than it would be to have dear old Don coming over three times a week to teach him how to dribble.

They went to a picnic area that was on a side road in a little canyon. Mark helped Don get the things out of the car, because his mother asked him to, but as soon as Don was busy building a fire and Mom was getting the food out of the picnic basket, Mark slipped away. He went down to the little river that ran through the campground. The water was shallow this time of year, and it rushed over the boulders that made up the riverbed. Mark followed the stream to a spot that was secluded, a place where the water pooled. There he picked up a stone and flipped it across the water, trying to make it skip, but the rock was too round, and he hadn't angled it just right. It plopped into the clear water and then wobbled as it sank into the dark bottom. He looked more carefully and found a flat rock. This he flipped the same way, except that he brought his arm lower, a deep side-arm, and the rock skipped twice before it sank like the other.

Mark looked for more good rocks, found several that were fairly flat and threw them all, each time counting the skips, trying to make them hop the way he had seen some boys make them do. But the little river wasn't very wide, and three or four hops was the best he could manage. He kept doing it, all the same, throwing over and over, dozens of times. It was engrossing, for some reason. He didn't think much about where he was or what he was doing, just kept throwing until after twenty minutes or so his arm began to get tired. He threw for a while longer anyway, but finally he sat down on a big rock near the edge of the water and just watched and listened.

The water swept into the pool, creating a slow swirling motion. Sticks or leaves floating along with the water made a wide arc along the riverbank and then picked up speed again as they emptied into the faster stream beyond. The sound of the faster water, a little downstream, and the sound of the breeze in the tall oak brush behind him seemed to blend into one. There were birds in the trees too, and gradually Mark became aware of them, especially a magpie that was chattering away. He liked this. He liked the sound, and he liked the pool that faded into darkness beneath the quiet surface. He was tempted to strip and dive in, but he knew the water came out of the mountains and was very cold; he also felt insecure about his swimming ability.

He wanted to stay here, not face Don and Mom again. Maybe they wouldn't look for him. He picked up some little rocks at his feet and lobbed them at the water, one at a time. They plopped on the serene surface and then gently slipped into the darker water. The circles spread out across the pond, concentric, perfect, until they gradually faded. He waited for each set of circles to disappear, then threw again. It was hypnotizing for some reason. Little water insects would sometimes slide across the water, into the circles, breaking the lines and creating their own patterns, and then ripples from the motion of the water would push the circles slowly downstream. Mark found it—something—maybe interesting, maybe pretty. But he didn't think about it; he didn't let himself. His whole life had become a calculated effort not to think, to occupy every moment with something distracting.

He heard the sound for some time before he let it sink into his consciousness. It was Don, calling, bellowing Mark's name, stretching out the vowel. Mark didn't move. He even stopped throwing the rocks, just sat quietly, listening. The sound did not come closer, but it persisted, on and on. What did it matter? He'd face them later and receive his mother's cold looks; that was better than being with the two of them all afternoon. The sound stopped eventually; then after a few minutes it came again, and this time it was much closer. Don had come to the river; he was upstream, but not far away. Mark hoped he would turn the wrong way, but he didn't. He soon called again, and he was obviously coming toward Mark. For an instant Mark thought of heading farther down the river, but then he gave up. It was pointless to try to hide. He stood and walked along the path toward Don.

"Oh, there you are," Don said. "Didn't you hear me?" There was an edge of irritation in his voice.

53

Mark didn't answer. He walked toward Don, but went on by him and continued toward the picnic area. He wanted the man to feel his hostility. He wanted there to be no question about it, so Don wouldn't keep bugging him about the basketball lessons.

"Listen, Mark, could I talk to you for just a minute?"

Mark stopped and turned back, taken by surprise. "Sure," he said, but he tried to make his voice flat.

"Have you decided not to like me?" Don had his hands on his hips. He was tall and fairly slender, except that he had a little too much fat around the middle, his stomach bulging a bit under his knit shirt. His voice sounded a little strained, but he was smiling. And there was something sort of disarming about his smile. His upper lip pulled up high, showing his gums, and his eyebrows seemed to jump up. It was a dumb, clownlike sort of grin in a way, but it was good-natured.

"No," Mark said, but he was embarrassed.

"Look, I'm not trying to push myself off on you. I understand about the basketball. I just thought maybe you wanted some help with your shooting. It doesn't matter to me either way." Mark nodded just a little. Don shifted his weight, and then he folded his arms across his chest. He was obviously nervous. "You know, Mark, I think I understand what you must be feeling. My parents were divorced, and my mother didn't ever marry again, but she used to go out with men once in a while, and to me it was always—well, you know, sort of difficult. So I . . . ah . . . think maybe I know what you might be thinking, or maybe feeling."

Mark would not say anything. He could see what the guy was up to, and he wasn't going to let it work. He looked away, down at the ground.

"So, anyway, I think we can get to know each other, gradually—but I won't push you or anything. You don't have to worry about that. I don't know whether your mother and I will. . . ." Mark suddenly looked up. "I mean, it's still too soon to, you know, decide anything about the future—or anything like that. But I guess you'll be seeing quite a bit of me, and . . . well . . . there's no reason for us to feel any . . . ah . . . or you know, to have trouble with each other."

Finally he just stopped. Mark was looking back at the ground by now, but he felt angry. He just wanted the big jerk to leave him alone. "We better go back," Mark mumbled as he turned and walked away. Don followed him, and said nothing more. In fact, the two hardly said a word to each other the rest of the afternoon. Mark spent some time throwing a Frisbee around with Ronnie, because his mother asked him to; but as soon as he could get away, he went back to the river and sat by the quiet pool.

That evening, when they got home, Don stayed around for a while. Mark took the chance, while Don and Mother were talking in the living room, to slip out the back door. He knew where he was going, but he pretended to himself that he was just wandering outside. He walked directly to Willard's and went in without knocking.

"Willard," he yelled, expecting the old man to be downstairs again.

"You don't need to yell so loud," Willard said, from a chair in the living room. "My hearing ain't quit on me yet."

"Oh, I thought you'd be downstairs. How come you're sitting in the dark?"

"Well, there ain't nothing to look at. I seen this room lots of times before. Might as well be in the dark as in the light, I guess."

Mark walked in and without asking sat down on the old couch across from Willard. His eyes were getting used to the semi-darkness, and he could see Willard fairly well.

"Don't you watch television or anything?"

"Oh sure. But the dang thing wears me out after a while. There ain't much on it worth watching. Except the ball games. I like to watch them. I watched most of the football game this afternoon."

"Was it any good?"

"Shoot, I don't know. I guess it was. I fell asleep halfway through the third quarter. I don't even know who won. Do you like football, Austin?"

"Not much."

"That's what you say about everything," Willard said, and he chuckled. "Is there anything you like?"

"I like music," Mark said. "At least *some* music."

"What, that rock stuff?"

"Yuh."

"I can't get nothing out of that stuff. It sounds just like a lot screaming to me—I can't understand the words."

"You wouldn't want to. The words are stupid anyway."

Willard laughed about that. "Some things never change, I guess," he said. And then he laughed quietly again, drawing air through his teeth. He was sitting in an old chair that had stuffing coming out along the arms, and he had the Sunday paper strewn around on the floor by his feet. He was wearing an old shabby pair of house slippers and his usual overalls. His face was hard to see clearly in the shadows, but Mark had the feeling he was not as happy as usual, even though he was laughing. He seemed sort of subdued.

"So what have you been doing today, Austin?"

"I went on a picnic with my mother and . . . a friend of hers."

"Have a good time?"

"No."

Willard laughed again. "How come?"

"I don't know. There was nothing to do up there."

"You gotta be the hardest kid to please in twenty counties, Austin. I'll bet you would've complained if your mother had made you stay home all day."

"No, I wouldn't," Mark said, but he smiled at Willard's teasing.

"Doesn't your mother make you go to church on Sunday?"

"No."

"Why not? What religion are you?"

"I'm not anything. I guess Mom went to church when she was a girl, but she hasn't gone for a long time, and my dad never did go. He always said religion was just a phony deal to get money out of people."

"So that's where you get that negative attitude of yours. Your old man taught it to you. What sort of guy was he anyway?"

Mark had been feeling pretty good, relaxed, but now he stiffened up. Willard never could seem to recognize what was none of his business. "He was mostly no good. That's what he was."

"What kind of work did he do?"

Mark wanted to get this stopped. "Mostly trying to sell different things. He was out of work half the time." But then he quickly added, "What religion are you, Willard?"

"I guess me and your dad was in the same church, Austin. I never have gone much either. I always fell asleep listening to those long-winded preachers." Willard stopped to cough. "But I do believe in God. I have to say that. And when you start to get old, like me, you start to give all that sort of thing a little more thought."

Mark couldn't think of a comment, so he finally said, "Why?"

"Well, I guess that's obvious. I ain't likely to be kicking around too much longer."

"Do you think there really is a heaven and all that, the way people say?"

"I don't know what there is, Austin." He sat for quite some time then, but Mark knew something more was coming and let the old man gather his thoughts. "I guess—now—I hope there's something. And I guess I hope that if there is, I won't be too bad off. But, see, I never thought about that when I was raising hell all those years. My wife always said I'd stop and think someday, and I guess she was right."

This was a topic Mark wanted to pursue. It was something he had done some thinking about. A lot of kids his age—especially in his other school—went to church. He had wondered about it and wondered what he believed, or whether he should believe anything at all. His dad's skepticism about religion had always impressed him, and he had enjoyed shocking other kids by saying he didn't believe in anything. But he didn't know. Sometimes he wondered about prayer. It would be a nice thing if it worked.

Willard was laughing quietly again. "You know what Gurney used to say?"

"Well, I'll bet he wasn't too religious."

"I guess I would have to say that's right—although his wife made him go to church plenty. But he used to say, 'I don't mind the preaching so much, and I can even put up with sitting on that old hard bench, but my wife thinks I ought to leave that church and go out and *do* all that stuff he preaches about—that's what gets my goat.' "

"What about McGill? Did he go to church?"

"Sure. Regular. Every year on Easter. And you know what he used to say about that?"

"Yuh, I'll bet he'd say, 'I went again this year, and the ol' church stood up to it again. I thought it might fall in this year.' "

"That's right, Austin. That's almost exactly what he'd say. You even got his voice about right."

"That's how you always do it—high like that."

"Yuh, I guess I do," Willard said. "I guess I talk about those old boys too much. I sure have missed them just lately."

A silence followed, and Mark felt sorry for Willard. They talked about this and that for quite some time before Mark went home. They didn't mention the trains, except that Willard did say he hoped Mark would come over and help him put on some more track. Mark said he would, but he wondered what in the world he was doing. Why was he hanging around with an old man? If the kids at school found out, they would never let him hear the end of it. Still, it was better than being home with Mom and Ronnie—and Don.

CHAPTER 6

Mark didn't go to Willard's on Monday or Tuesday. In some ways he wanted to, but he hated to have Willard start to expect him all the time. Besides, he still had had some of the money from Friday night, so he had been able to go to the arcade in the afternoons.

All day Wednesday Mark felt tired. The night before, the words had started repeating themselves while he was asleep, and he had even seen his dad in a dream. He had awakened scared and upset, and he hadn't gotten back to sleep for quite a while. Even at school, he found himself fighting all day not to hear the words, and this worried him. He had always thought they would go away gradually, if he just waited and tried to control himself, but they seemed to be pressing in on him more often instead of less. He felt almost sick by the time he went to his American history class that afternoon.

Mr. Sampson gave the class a reading assignment and let them use class time for it. He did that quite often; he was the laziest teacher Mark knew. Mark got out his book and stared at the words on the page, but they never passed into his head. He kept glancing up at the girl across from him and one seat ahead. All he knew about her was that her name was Andrea. But she was pretty, with dimples and nice skin. Sometimes he thought about going to an afternoon dance and asking her to dance with him, but it bothered him that she was a little taller than he was, and he also didn't know what he could say to her. He figured he could fake the dancing part, since everyone just sort of hopped around anyway; it was the talking that scared him.

"Mark, use this time to get your reading done, all right?" Mark looked up to see Mr. Sampson standing not far away, looking down at him. "Lord knows you won't take it home."

Mark said nothing, simply moved his eyes over to the page. But some of the kids laughed. Mark glanced up for just a second and saw that Andrea was looking back at him. She was smiling. One of her girl friends had told Mark that Andrea was sort of interested in him—and she did always say "hi" in the hallways. But he wondered what she was thinking now. She was a good student. She probably thought he was just a goof-off. He tried to tell himself that he really didn't care.

Looking back at the book, Mark felt himself sinking deeper inside his own head. It scared him. The words always came when he was most alone. He liked to be doing something that took his whole attention. During the rest of the class period the time passed like dripping honey, and he was all shaky inside when the bell finally rang.

He was up the aisle and out of the class before most of the kids had even moved. Only one more class, and then he could escape the trap for another day. His last class was Spanish, which he didn't mind too much, because the teacher was a young guy who kidded around quite a bit and gave them almost no homework.

He got to class a little early, but he went in and sat down. Whittington was in the class too. When he came in, he walked past Mark, sort of glanced at him but said nothing, and went by. Then he stopped and came back. "Hey, Austin," he said.

Mark twisted around and looked up from his desk. "You know that old guy who lives down the street from you—the one we always kid around with?"

"Yuh."

"What's his name, do you know?"

"No." Mark felt himself getting nervous. "Why?"

"I just wondered. It'd probably blow his mind if we started to call him by his real name." Mark didn't respond. He was afraid to say anything at all.

The girl who sat across the aisle from Mark had just come in. "Why don't you guys leave that old man alone?" she said. She looked at both of them as though she were including Mark.

"Shut up, Debbie," Whittington said. "It's none of your business."

"Shut up yourself, Larry," she said. It was the first time Mark had ever heard Whittington's first name. "I think you guys are rotten. How would you like a bunch of stupid kids calling you 'gramps' and yelling at you every day like that?"

"Oh, crap. It's probably the biggest thrill he gets in his life. I'll bet he comes out there and waits for us, just so he can get some attention for a while."

Debbie sat down, setting her books in front of her, but she didn't take her eyes off Whittington. She was a fairly small girl who usually didn't say all that much. Mark was amazed at the way she was standing up to Whittington. "Yuh, sure," she said, "and that's why he just sits there and stares back at you guys like that. Can't you tell that it makes him feel bad?"

"Debbie, like I said before, shut up. If you think I care what you think, you're nuts. It's not like we're hurting the old guy. We don't go over there and *do* anything to him."

"How would you like someone yelling like that at your grandfather? Have you thought about it that way?" But Whittington only waved his hand in disgust.

That set Mark to wondering about Willard. Just how much did these guys bother him?

"Anyway, Austin," Whittington said, "why don't you see if you can find out what his name is?"

Mark sort of shook his head, but he still didn't speak.

"What?"

"Look, Whittington, I've got better things to do with my time than wander around trying to find out what some old guy's name is."

"Like what? What do you do with your precious time, Austin? I never see you doing anything."

Mark turned back toward his desk, avoiding Whittington's eyes. What he wanted to do was punch him right in his lumpy gut. "What I do is my own business," he finally said.

"Look, what would it hurt to just ask some neighbor what the guy's name is? Or what about your parents—they probably know." Mark didn't say anything. More of the kids were coming in now, and one of the guys was up at the blackboard, apparently trying to write some message in Spanish. Whittington stepped up closer to Mark's desk. "Won't you even ask someone?"

"No."

"Gees, Austin, what a little creep you are. Maybe I'll take you out and pound your head in after school tonight—then we'll see if you won't do it."

Mark looked up. "Look, Whittington, just take a hike, all right? If you want to find out the guy's name so much, why don't *you* go ask someone?"

Mr. Knowles walked into the room, and Whittington glanced at him, then said to Mark, under his breath, "You're going to wish you hadn't talked that way to me."

As Whittington walked back to his desk, Debbie nodded at Mark. This was apparently a sign that she approved of what he had done, but it didn't help much. Mark figured he would get smashed as soon as school was out. All the same, when the class was over, he didn't try to hide. He walked out slower than usual and strolled down to his locker, expecting Whittington to come up behind him at any moment. Mark knew he could never handle a guy that big, but he was going to get in a few shots before he was finished off. It was almost satisfying—exciting—to think of doing it.

But Whittington didn't show up in the hallway; and while everyone waited for the bus, he was there with his friend Anders and he didn't pay any attention to Mark. It wasn't until they all got on the bus, and Mark had already sat down, that Whittington came up to him. "Say, Austin," he said, "Anders and I have decided to sit in this seat. So get up and move like a nice little boy."

"Take a hike," Mark said, and then he looked out the window. Inside he was shaking, and it was hard to look away, because he didn't know what might be coming.

"Sonny boy, you have said that to me twice today. And it's not nice for little boys to say things like that. You get up now, or you will be sorry." Anders was laughing, and several other guys on the bus came back to see what was going on. They were standing in the aisle, stretching to see over each other.

Mark didn't move. He didn't say anything either. He knew that Whittington couldn't just stand there and keep asking, because that would make him look stupid. But he also knew that Whittington wouldn't want to start a fight on the bus, with the driver sitting up front. That would mean certain suspension from school. Whittington wasn't that brave.

Suddenly Whittington reached out and grabbed Mark's arm, just below the elbow. Mark drove his arm forward, releasing himself, but Whittington had him around the neck with his other arm before Mark could fight him off. He locked his arm around his neck and tried to drag him out of the seat, but Mark grabbed the seat in front of himself and held on, struggling to pull his head free. The scuffling brought a reaction from the boys close by, and Anders said, "Get 'im," loudly enough that the bus driver apparently realized something was going on.

"Hey, stop that," he yelled. Whittington let go immediately and ducked into the seat behind Mark. "What's the trouble?" the driver said. But by the time he came back through the bus, everyone was finding a seat. Mark was still alone, however, and his hair was all messed up. "Were you in on this?" the driver said, pointing at Mark. Mark didn't answer. "Were you?"

"In on what?"

The driver stared at him for a moment, and then he looked around, trying to figure out who else had been involved. "I'll have no fighting on this bus," he said, after a time. "I hope you guys all heard that." He was sounding as tough as he could, but he was not very frightening. He went back to his seat, and the guys around Mark started to laugh.

"You're going to pay yet," Whittington whispered from the seat behind. "Did you hear me, little boy?"

No one sat by Mark, but that was usually the case when the bus wasn't full. He dreaded the ride home now. Whittington probably wouldn't get off with him at his stop—the big slob was too lazy for that. But what Mark hated was passing Willard's place. On both Monday and Tuesday Willard had been out there on the porch. Mark had sat on the opposite side so that Willard wouldn't watch him go by and maybe wave at him. It seemed odd, though, that he wasn't downstairs working on the train.

Willard was out on the porch again today. Whittington and Anders, and some of the other guys, spread it on thick. "Hey, gramps, don't overdo it now. Don't wear yourself out sitting in that chair."

"Grandpa, what're yuh doing? Thinking about the good old days?"

Whittington had gotten up and crossed the aisle. He leaned over a couple of guys and yelled, "You shouldn't sit so much, gramps. You're going to get hemorrhoids if you're not careful." This got a bigger laugh than usual. Mark could see that even some of the girls up front were laughing.

"Sit down, Whittington," the bus driver yelled, but Mark could tell that Whittington wasn't worried. Mark glanced at Willard a couple of times. He was showing no reaction, just looking back at the boys. Mark looked out the other window and tried not to listen, tried not to think. The house across the street needed paint, and the one next to it needed a lot more than that. A kid with his diaper hanging halfway off was out in front, crying, just standing on the sidewalk all by himself. What a lousy day!

CHAPTER 7

M ark went into his house for just a minute or
two, then he walked down to Willard's. Willard was still sitting out on the porch. "Hello, Austin,"
he said, as Mark approached, but he looked solemn.
He had on his usual old faded overalls, but he didn't
look quite his usual self. His face seemed sort of pale,
and his eyes looked deeper and darker than they ever
had before.

"Hi," Mark said. He went up on the porch. There
was only the one chair, the one Willard was using,
but Mark sat on the rail that ran across the front of

the porch. On either side of him was the wild-looking climbing rosebush.

"How yuh doing, Austin?" Willard said, but he didn't look directly at him.

"Okay." Mark wanted to say the right thing, but he had no idea how to start. "Willard, those guys on the bus are a bunch of idiots."

"It don't matter," Willard said. That was all. And Mark couldn't think of anything else to say. The two of them just sat for a time. They didn't even look at each other. Willard had leaned forward, with his elbows on his knees.

"Willard, it's only about four guys who think that kind of stuff is funny."

"I said it don't matter, Austin." Willard sounded irritated, but in a moment he said, "I thought you was coming over this week to work on the train."

"Well, I couldn't make it." Mark hated his stupid lies sometimes. "We can work on it now, though. If you want to."

"There's a lot of that stuff I can't reach," Willard said, still looking down.

"Well, let's go down. I have some time right now. I'll have to go check on Ronnie in a little while, but that won't take long."

Once again Willard took his time before he answered. "I don't know," he finally said. "I'm thinking about forgetting the whole thing. It just costs a lot of money and takes a lot of time."

"Why did you start it then, Willard?"

"I don't know. It was just something . . . I don't know."

"It was just what?"

Willard looked up at Mark. He was squinting, and deep lines were drawn in around his eyes. He sucked at the back of his teeth. "It was just one of those things that stupid old fools get into their heads sometimes. I couldn't start to explain it to you."

Mark didn't say anything. He felt confused. Why was he mixed up with this man's problems, his old age, his sadness? There was no way he could help. But he did feel sorry for him. In a way, he wanted to do something. "I think I understand," he finally said. He knew he was lying, and he suspected that Willard knew it too, but he felt almost good about saying it.

"I bought another train," Willard said, after a time. "It's a little old steam locomotive with mostly coal cars. It's for the run up to the mine from the little mining town."

"Does it make it up those hills all right?"

"I don't know, Austin. I've had so much pain in my back lately that I couldn't get under the board to get back to where I could set it out."

"When did you get it, Willard?"

"Monday."

Mark knew now why Willard had been on the porch every afternoon, and he suddenly felt ashamed. But he didn't know what to say. "Let's go down and put it on then. Okay?"

"If we start again, I need to have you come more often. I'm in sort of a hurry."

"Hurry? Why, Willard?"

Willard looked at Mark carefully, as though he were trying to judge what he should say, as though there were something he wanted to say, but then he glanced away. "I like to get a job finished when I start it," he said. "I don't like to just piddle along."

"All right. I'll come over every night that I can. I can almost always come right after school for a while."

Willard nodded, and then he got up slowly, straightening his back only a little at a time. His face tightened, and his eyes squinted. He was breathing hard.

"Are you all right?" Mark asked.

"No. I'm older than hell." He still looked strained, but he began to chuckle, his breath coming in little jerks.

The two of them went downstairs, but Willard had to take the steps very slowly. Mark thought about helping him, but he was too embarrassed to do anything like that.

Willard had done a little work on the train, but mostly in the yard up front. He had finished the tracks there, and he had spread some stuff along them that looked like real dirt and cinders. And he had set out a little mail wagon with a figure of a man by it.

The new train was parked in the yard too, but Mark knew where it was supposed to go. He ducked under the board to the central control area, and then he carefully uncoupled the locomotive. He took it to the back and reached across far enough to place it on the upper track. And then, one car at a time, he moved the whole train up to the other track. When he had it all lined up and ready, he looked around to Willard. "Which lever controls this line?"

"The one in the middle, on this panel over here."

Mark moved the lever down, just a little, and the old steam engine started to chug. "Hey, Willard, listen to it," Mark said.

"I know. It sounds real, don't it? I already run it a little down here on the main line."

"Do I have to stop it when it gets to the end of the line?"

"Nope. It comes to a stop, automatic. And then if you just leave it, after a minute it starts up by itself and runs down to the town. Then it does the same thing down there."

"How does it do that?"

"Well, that's how it's wired. I done that before, when I first set it all up. But now we got us a lot better train."

"It's a beauty," Mark said, and Willard nodded. The two of them watched while it sat at the mine, by the coal loader, and then, just as Willard had said it would, it started by itself and chugged back down the long hill toward the town. "That's really all right," Mark said. He looked around at Willard, who was standing by the front of the board. He was nodding, smiling a little. He looked a lot better.

Mark pulled the lever down that started the other train, the Sante Fe, and it rolled out of the yard and onto the main line. As it looped into the first tunnel, Mark said, "We need to get that track finished at the far end, don't we? So we can switch out of the main line into the other loop."

"That's right," Willard said. "But I can hardly reach any of that."

"I'll get it," Mark said, but first he watched the train finish its run back into the yard and then he shut it down. "Well, Gurney," he said, pitching his voice high, "we gotta have this engine worked over and ready by quitting time, so we better be getting at 'er."

"Shoot, McGill," Willard said, "it ain't going nowhere till we're finished with it anyhow—so what's the big hurry?"

"Don't you take no pride in turning out a job on time, Gurney?"

Willard was laughing now. "You're getting that down, you know that, Austin? That's just about how them two talked, except it was Gurney who worked the hardest, not McGill. Ol' McGill, he figured things would get done sooner or later, but Gurney always pushed a little more—not that he kill't himself."

"I guess I'll get started on that track," Mark said. He started gathering up the things he would need.

"All right. I'm afraid I can't be too much help today. But I'm going to work on some new trees. I bought some of them kind that you make yourself— you can shape 'em any way you want."

"Aren't you spending too much, Willard?" Mark asked. "You bought a bunch of stuff."

Willard stopped for a moment. He looked rather serious again. "I have my retirement money—from the railroad—and I've saved some money. I figure I might as well spend it on this as on anything else."

"But what if you need it later? Mom's always telling us we have to leave some money in the bank—in case we have to have it some time."

Willard looked out across the board, his breath coming steadily, audibly. "Well, your mother is right. But I guess I've got enough for my needs."

"Is something the matter, Willard?"

"There sure is, McGill." His voice was low and sort of boisterous. "My body's quitting on me, but my memory's just fine." He grinned at Mark.

"Well, Gurney," Mark said, trying to do McGill's voice, "I'm worse off than you. I'm all raring to go— and feeling just fine—but I can't remember where I'm supposed to go."

Willard laughed until he coughed. It was some time before he could get his breath enough to say, "Austin, you're some kid. I swear, that's just exactly the kind of thing ol' McGill used to say all the time."

Mark went to work on the track, and Willard fiddled with trees over at the workbench. But Mark didn't think much about the time, and before he realized it, it was almost seven o'clock. He had never even checked on Ronnie.

"Oh, gees," he said, when he did notice. "Willard,

I've got to go. My mom's going to be mad. It's past time for dinner."

"All right, you go on. Are you coming tomorrow?"

"Yuh. Unless Mom gets mad and says I can't." He was heading for the stairs.

"Wait, Austin. Let me pay you. You been here for over three hours."

"That's all right, Willard. You don't need to pay me."

"All right. But keep track of your hours, and I'll pay you at the end of the week."

"No. That's not what I mean. I'll keep coming over, but don't pay me anymore, okay?" He didn't wait for an answer, just hurried up the stairs. He didn't want to talk to Willard about this.

When he got home, his mother was obviously upset, but she didn't say too much right at first. Don had come for dinner and was still there. Dinner was over, and the two of them were washing the dishes together. Mark suddenly felt changed, all stone inside. He didn't want this guy in his kitchen washing dishes and looking right at home.

"Where have you been?" his mother asked. She obviously was straining not to sound angry, but Mark could hear the tenseness. Mark only shrugged. He was not going to talk about Willard in front of Don. "Were you at the arcade?"

"No."

"Mark, tell me the truth."

Mark's temper flashed. "I was *not* at the arcade—

and don't call me a liar." He walked into his bedroom and slammed the door behind him. Just a few minutes before, he had felt good, happy even, and now this! He dropped onto his bed and turned the radio on.

Soon after his mother came in and told him that there were a couple of pork chops in the oven and some rice. She was going to a movie with Don. "Can you look after Ronnie?"

"Yuh."

"Sit up and look at me, Mark."

Mark didn't move immediately, but eventually he rolled over and sat up. He tried to make his look as defiant as possible. "All right, I'm looking at you."

"I'm sorry I accused you like that," she said. "But it's still true that you were *hours* late coming home, and that you missed dinner completely." Mark was closing in, shutting her out. He just stared at her. "I am your mother, and I deserve some respect. I want you to tell me where you were."

Mark continued to stare at her. Fifteen or twenty very long seconds went by, but Mark didn't answer. "All right, Mark, consider yourself grounded. For the next week I want you to come home directly after school and—"

"No, Mom. Wait." Mark stood up. "Okay, I was working. Honest. I was working for someone."

"Who were you working for, Mark?" She still seemed not to believe him, but Mark couldn't let his anger show now. He couldn't stand the thought of being grounded. Being home alone in the house every afternoon for a week would be intolerable. He had to have something to keep him busy.

"I was helping Mr. Willard."

"The old man down the street?"

"Yes."

"Mark, he can't afford to pay anyone—he—"

"I know, Mom. I know. I'm not taking any money from him anymore. I'm just helping him out with some things."

When his mother didn't speak for a time, Mark finally looked at her again. She was obviously puzzled, and yet a softness had returned to her face, her mouth no longer tight. "All right, Mark. I'd like to know more about this, but I have to go now. From now on, don't come home so late. And don't leave Ronnie alone so long. All right?"

Mark nodded. His mother left, and he lay back down on the bed. He didn't feel like eating yet. He hadn't given in to his mother like that in a long time. In a way he felt defeated. But he also felt some sense of relief.

CHAPTER 8

||||||||||||||||||||||||||||||||||||||||||||||||||||||||||||||||

Mark was expecting big troubles at school the next day. But as it turned out, Whittington walked by in the hallway, seemed to look right through Mark, and didn't say a word. He was with some of his buddies, laughing and talking, and he seemed not to care about what had happened. He yelled his usual insults at Willard's house that afternoon, and then, when Mark was getting off the bus, he shouted out, "Hey, little fellow, don't forget, I still have a score to settle with you." So it semed to Mark that he was more interested in looking tough in front of his friends than he was in actually fighting.

Mark waited for the bus to clear the neighborhood and then hurried over to Willard's house. Willard was downstairs. He hadn't done too much on the track, but he had obviously been puttering around down there for a while. "Hey, Gurney," Mark said, "if you don't get a little more work done, I'm going to have to tell the boss you been sitting down on the job."

Willard was standing, bent forward a little. He turned and smiled at Mark, pushing his hair back out of his eyes at the same time, but he never really straightened up. "Shoot, McGill, you should talk. I've been down here all day, and here you are just showing up for work."

Mark walked over to Willard and stood close to him. At school that day he had thought about some dumb things he could have McGill say. "Well, I know, Gurney, but my wife had another baby today."

"Another one already?"

"Yup. But this one's the best looking one in the whole litter. It has two eyes and just one nose—it ain't at all like my other kids."

Willard obviously thought that was a good one. He shook his head and laughed, and then he put his hand on Mark's shoulder. "McGill, you mean to tell me some of your kids is a little strange?"

"Well, Gurney, I hate to call 'em that, you know, since they're my own flesh and blood—but I have to admit, that oldest daughter of mine is a little out of the ordinary."

"Well, I don't know. Sure she has the nine fingers

on each hand. But you see folks like that ever' once in a while."

Mark was grinning now. "No, it ain't the fingers I worry about. I figure the more of them the better. At least I know when she takes hold of something, she's got it. It's her toes I worry about."

"You mean she has nine of them, too?"

"Oh no. She's just got the regular six on each foot, like all my kids. But they're so dang long, Gurney. They're the ugliest things I ever seen." Mark hesitated, for the sake of the right timing, and then he came back with his high-pitched voice. "She went out on the porch the other morning without her shoes on. The milkman come along and thought he'd got himself in a herd of rattlesnakes. He dropped four quarts of milk getting out of there."

Willard laughed in his breathy way, shaking his head and patting Mark's shoulder. "You're as bad as McGill, I swear," he said.

"Shoot, Gurney, let's quit this fooling around and get down to some serious work on this here train."

"Well, all right, McGill, but you better give her a try, just to see if she'll run. Can you drive one of these here trains?"

"I guess I can. I can do most everything—I can't see why I can't do something as easy as drive a train down a track. It can't be so hard as driving a car."

"Well, then, let 'er rip." Mark stooped and got under the board and into the opening in the center. There he pushed down the levers that started both trains. And only then did he notice that there was a new train on the board. It was on the main line, and it was the one that pulled out of the yard. It was a nice one too, a Union Pacific with a yellow and red engine and lots of cars. Back behind, the little coal train came chugging down the hill. Mark let the new train run all the way around the board once, and then when it came around the second time, he switched it onto the track that took the wider loop around the end, passing on the outside of the mining town. But then, when he brought it back around and into the yard, he brought it to a stop. "Now, how do I get the other one—the Santa Fe—back onto the main run?" It was sitting on another track in the yard.

"What's the matter, McGill? I thought you knew this yard. Throw that switch—the second one over—on this panel over here." He pointed to the panel. Mark threw the switch, and then pulled the Santa Fe out of the yard and took it around a couple of times. When he brought it back in, Willard said, "I suppose we ought to bring it in and service it, but the track ain't ready yet. We can't get it across to the turntable and into the roundhouse."

Mark was confused for a moment. "What do you mean, Willard? Do we have to service it already?"

Willard looked up from the board. "Oh, no. Not these trains. I just meant—you know—Gurney might say something like that.

"Oh, yuh." Mark stood for a moment. He was embarrassed, and he knew Willard was too. "Well,

Gurney, we'll just have to give her a once-over right here in the yard. She needs oiling, don't she?"

"She sure does. That's a long run you had her on."

But neither could look at each other. Mark wondered what the heck he was doing. "Maybe what we better do is get that track down. Then we can pull her in and fix her up right."

Willard agreed, so Mark got things organized and went to work on the track. Willard still had some trees to work on. He had already made up a couple dozen of them, but Mark could see that he had quite a few more to do.

And so they worked and talked about the layout and the new train, and the other one Willard had seen and wanted to buy. Mark left once to check on Ronnie, but when he came back, they picked up where they had left off. They slipped in and out of Gurney and McGill's voices without thinking much about it anymore. Eventually Willard came closer to the board and watched Mark. "How's she coming, McGill?" he said.

"Not bad, Gurney. Except I took my finger for a railroad tie and almost shortened it up a little."

"Did you cut yourself?"

"Not too bad. Just a little. Back in the war I was hurt a lot worse than that. Once I got my finger caught in a typewriter and almost ripped it right off." Willard laughed, but Mark felt strange for a moment. He knew who used to say that.

Mark worked for a while longer, and then he went home to dinner. But he told Willard he would come back afterwards. And he did hurry back, avoiding his mother's questions about what kind of work he had been doing. When he got back, he found Willard in the living room. "What are you up to, Gurney? Can't I leave for a minute without you goofing off on the job?"

But Willard didn't respond in Gurney's big voice. He only said, "I fixed me a little something to eat, Austin. Then I had to sit down. I guess I've been on my feet too long today."

"Does your back hurt?" Mark sat down on the couch, across from Willard.

"No more than the rest of me."

"Are you getting sick or something?"

Willard didn't say anything at first. He looked at Mark rather seriously, the way he had on the porch the day before. "I'm getting old," he said. "That's what I'm getting."

"No you're not, Willard," Mark said, trying to look quite serious. "You *are* old."

Willard nodded and smiled, and then he reached up and pushed the fine white hair back from his forehead, back along his big ears. "Well, I'll tell you one thing, Austin," he said. "You're going to get yourself in the same fix—and it comes on you a whole lot faster than you'd ever expect."

"Is it bad?"

"What?"

"I mean, is it really so bad to be old?"

"Yuh, I guess in most ways it's bad. Your body slows down and it starts to hurt more, and it gets tired easy. You fall asleep all day, and then you can't go to sleep at night. And everybody starts to treat you differ'nt."

"What do you mean?"

"I don't know. They nod and smile if you start talking to them, but you know what they're thinking: 'I gotta get away before this old guy takes up too much of my valuable time.' "

Mark had never thought much about old age. Old people were just grandmas and grandpas. And they were always happy, he thought. But Mark looked at old Willard now. He saw the loose skin hanging from his neck, the broken little red lines across his cheek and nose, and the white circles edging the pupils of his eyes. He was so ugly. It had never really struck Mark before that he, himself, was in the process of coming to look like that. He suddenly felt uncomfortable and wanted to leave.

"I'll tell you when it first hit me just how old I was. It was a few years ago when it really come clear to me." He looked down at his hands and rubbed them together. He had big hands, but thin, and the fingers were all bone. "I don't go down to the park much any more, but when I used to, when Gurney and McGill was still alive, sometimes young folks—teenagers and college kids—would be out there throwing those things around. Them disks. What do you call 'em?"

"Frisbees?"

"Yuh. They'd be throwing them around and running and catching them. Well, one time I got down there before any of my friends, and I was just sitting there watching a couple of young girls throwing those things. They just had on short pants and little ol' T-shirts. And I want to tell you, boy, they looked awful pretty." But then he hesitated, still looking down, as though he were doubtful as to what he wanted to say. "So anyway, this one girl was running after the thing one time and it floated over to me, almost hit me in the leg. I just picked it up and handed it to her when she come over to me. Well, she stopped and told me thanks, and then she said it was a nice day and I said it sure was. I never seen a girl so pretty, Austin."

He looked at Mark, as though he expected him to understand, but Mark was mainly embarrassed. He hated to hear old Willard talk that way.

"So anyway, I guess she wanted a rest, and she stood and talked to me for a little while. The other girl come over too, and we just said something about the weather or something of that kind. But she was still breathing hard, and she just stood there with her hands on her hips and the wind blowing her pretty hair around. It was an awful thing for me, Austin. I don't know if you can understand that." Mark refused to look at him. "When she left, she reached out and patted me on the knee and said it was nice to talk to me or something like that. And it didn't worry her one bit to touch me like that. Because I was just an old man—not anyone to have any fear of."

Willard stopped. Mark finally looked up. Willard had leaned over, his elbows on his knees. "I'm an old fool," he finally said. "But, Austin, there was a time when I guess I was pretty nice-looking. I guess I was even a bit of a lady's man."

"At least you have something to remember," Mark said. "Girls don't look at me at all." He really didn't want to talk about this either.

"What are you talking about, Austin? You're a good-looking boy. You have those dark eyes and such thick hair. You're just getting your growth a little late, that's all. But when you get it, the girls will take notice of you."

"That's a laugh, Willard. Girls don't even know I exist. Nobody does."

"Well, that's what you've chosen, Austin. You know that."

"I don't know what you're talking about," Mark said, and felt himself closing up.

"Shoot, don't give me that. You wear them old shirts everyday, and you don't ever comb your hair, and you don't say a word to nobody. I see you sitting by yourself on that bus."

"I can't help it if no one wants to sit by me."

"Come on, Austin. That's not true, and you know it. You could make friends if you wanted to."

"You sound like my mother," Mark said, in the tone that he used with his mother. He stood up. "Look, I better get going."

Willard looked up at him, his eyes drawn into narrow pockets. "Listen, Austin. You don't have time to be like that. Life ain't so long as you think it is. It ain't long enough to waste *any* of it."

Mark walked to the door. "I'll come over tomorrow," he said. And then, in McGill's voice, "I gotta get back to all them screaming kids."

"Ain't I right?"

"No," Mark said. "I can't help it if people don't like me. I'm new at this school."

"You just keep making up excuses like that, Austin. One of these days you'll be hobbling around like me and wondering why you messed up your whole life."

Mark took a breath and held on for a moment. "Look, Willard. There's something. . . . There's something . . . else. But I can't talk about it. Let's just do the trains together, all right?" He didn't wait for an answer. Just left. But when he got to the porch, for a moment he seriously considered going back in. But he couldn't do it. He went home.

CHAPTER 9

A couple of weeks went by, and Mark was at Willard's nearly every day. He hardly went to the arcade at all anymore. The train layout was really shaping up. The track was all on, and the mountains and towns were gradually being refurbished. Willard, however, was doing less and less of the work. His back was hurting him so badly that he often simply had to sit and give instructions. But more and more, Mark knew what had to be done and just went ahead, conversing with Willard as he worked, or more often than not, with Gurney. They had gradually fallen into assuming the other voices almost from the moment Mark arrived. Sometimes they even discussed plans for the trains in the same voices, without bothering to switch back. The nice thing about it was that when Mark was McGill, he didn't have to answer for Mark; he didn't even have to think about Mark.

Actually, Mark never really came to care all that much about the trains or the layout, but he liked the preoccupation they provided. He was having more trouble at night now, sometimes not being able to go to sleep, or awakening long before it was time to get up. As often as not, he didn't even hear the words; he just felt with a terrible anxiety that they were in his head somewhere, waiting.

What Mark was not doing at all was his schoolwork. First term grades were coming up, and teachers were starting to get serious, dropping little warnings and reminding students of what work had to be finished before grades went in. Mrs. Pederson called Mark up to her desk after school one day and asked him if he knew that he was flunking. Mark just sort of shrugged.

"I don't understand, Mark," she said. "The work you get done in class is usually correct. But you never bother to finish your assignments. I know that you're smart enough to get good grades, if you'd just give it a little effort." Mark used the technique that he had perfected in recent months. He simply said nothing. "Mark, I checked your elementary school records. You consistently scored well ahead of your own grade level on achievement tests, not just in math but in everything, and you got good grades. You did the same thing at the other junior high last year. What's going on this year?"

"I don't know," Mark said, quickly and softly.

"I'm going to call your parents in for a conference, Mark. And I want one of our school counselors to be there too. You are never a behavior problem, but you're working so far below your ability that it's clear the problem is with your motivation." Mark still didn't comment. Mrs. Pederson was getting nervous. She was a fair-skinned woman, with red hair, but now the color in her face was rising. "I'll call your parents tonight," she said. "You can go now."

Mark hated to think of the little speeches that would be coming from his mother now—and the conference, with everyone trying to analyze him. When he got to his locker that afternoon, he gave some thought to taking his math home and doing some work, just to get everyone off his back. But he looked at the book for a few seconds and then slammed the locker door with a clang that echoed up and down the hallway. It was Friday, and all he wanted was to forget school for two full days.

When he went outside, the wind was blowing and clouds were rolling overhead. It was starting to feel more like winter all the time. Mark waited by the school, staying out of the wind as much as he could. A guy from his Spanish class came by and said hello. He even stopped and made some comment about their teacher, but Mark didn't say much in response. The kid—Mark thought his name was Jeff—had been friendly a couple of times before, and Mark really wanted to respond. But there was nothing in him right now, and he just couldn't bring himself to make the effort. The guy made another comment, and when Mark didn't say anything, he looked uncomfortable and walked away.

Mark was not far from the stairs when Whittington came out the door with Anders and a couple of other eighth-graders. "There's Austin, your little buddy," one of the guys said to Whittington.

"Hey, yuh, Austin," Whittington said. "I want to talk to you. I thought you said you didn't know that old guy's name." Mark didn't answer. "Skip Carmichael lives across the street from that guy, and he said he's seen you going over there after school. He said you walk right in the old guy's house without even knocking."

"Carmichael doesn't know what he's talking about," Mark said, but he was sorry as soon as he spoke. He should have just told Whittington the truth.

"Look, Austin, he *saw* you. What are you, some kind of weirdo—hanging around with an old guy like that?"

"Yuh," Anders said, "it sounds a little sick, if you ask me."

"Shut up, Anders," Mark said. Anders grabbed for him, but Whittington already had him, his hands gripping Mark's jacket.

"Look, little punk," Whittington said, "you're lucky in a way that you're so small. If you were more my size, I'd break your head open."

"Go ahead and try, bozo," Mark said. He was expecting to get murdered, but it was worth it.

"Go ahead and give it to him, Whittington," one of the guys said. "He's asking for it."

Whittington let go with one hand and cuffed Mark across the side of the head. It stung Mark's ear. "I ought to," he said. "I really ought to."

"I'll do it if you don't," Anders said. He pushed in closer to Whittington. A little crowd had begun to gather.

"All right, Austin," Whittington said, "I'll tell you what. Tell me what the old man's name is, and I'll let you go."

"Forget it," Mark said. "Ask Carmichael, if he knows so much." Mark could see more kids gathering all the time; he was humiliated.

"Carmichael doesn't know. I asked him. But *you* know. You're the little pervert that goes over there." He pulled Mark up, abruptly, so that he was standing on his toes. "He must be the only friend you can find. Now tell me what his name is."

Mark didn't answer. After a few seconds Whittington slapped him across the side of the head again, this time harder. "Tell me now, or you'll wish you'd never seen the old guy."

Mark still didn't speak, and he took another blow,

but he could see kids starting to move aside, and he knew that teachers must be coming.

"What's going on over there?" someone asked. Whittington let go and tried to step into the crowd. "Whittington, are you in on this?" It was the assistant principal.

Anders spoke up. "It's Austin here who started the trouble, Mr. Boyd. He's just lucky he's such a little shrimp or we might have let him have it."

Mr. Boyd looked skeptical. He looked from one boy to the other, trying to perceive what had been going on. "Who's Austin?" Anders pointed to Mark. "Is that right, Austin?" Mark just stared at the man. What a stupid game. "Is that right?"

"If Anders says so, it must be right," Mark said, with acid in his voice. "I know he wouldn't tell a lie."

"You have a smart mouth, little boy." He pointed his finger at Mark. "No wonder you get yourself in trouble. One of these days there won't be anyone around to save your skin, and one of these bigger boys will put some of your teeth out." Mark glared at the man, but he didn't say anything. "All right, everyone clear out of here."

Mark's bus was pulling up, and Whittington and his buddies took off running, making sure they got the seats they liked, the ones near the back and on Willard's side of the street. Mark ended up getting on almost last. He had to take a seat near the middle of the bus, next to a ninth-grade guy he had seen around but didn't know. From the back of the bus the guys were all shouting, "You have a smart mouth, little boy." Mark didn't move, didn't look back, but he hated. He hated the stupid assistant principal, and he hated Whittington and Anders. He hated Mrs. Pederson. He hated the school. He hated his life. He hated himself. He wished that he had driven his fist into Whittington's face, even if it had just been once.

The guy next to him said, "Don't let those jerks get you down." He was a big guy, a Spanish-American kid who was a foot taller than Mark. Mark hated him, too. He didn't want the guy's pity.

What made things worse was that Willard was out on the porch. He had been there more lately, since it was harder for him to work on the trains. "Hey, gramps," Whittington bellowed, "wave to your little buddy, Austin. He'll be right over to see you." His huge voice filled the bus.

The driver, rather lamely, yelled over his shoulder, "Shut up and sit down, Whittington," but no one paid any attention.

"Hey, grandpa," Anders was yelling. "I hope you and Austin have a swell time together. Be sure to tell him some stories about the good ol' days."

Mark was breathing hard, but he wouldn't look at Willard, and he wouldn't look back. He stared at the seat in front of him, and he knew that the girl across the aisle was watching him. "Those guys are sick," she said. "Don't listen to them." Mark didn't look at her.

"Don't worry, gramps," Whittington shouted, "he'll be right over. You're the only friend he has, you know."

The bus rolled on by, and then came to a stop at the corner. Mark was already up, moving toward the front. "Austin, try to control yourself. I know you can't wait to get over to your old buddy's place." Whittington was laughing, his voice rattling through the bus. Mark wanted to run—but he walked, self-consciously, slowly, never looking to either side. As the bus moved on, Anders had his head out the window. "Now don't make ol' gramps wait, Austin. You're the joy of his life."

Mark didn't look at the bus. His face was hot. His eyes were burning. He went into the house and into his room, shut the door, pulled back his bedspread and put his pillow in the middle of his bed. He looked at it for a few seconds. Then he drove his fist into it. He struck it again and again, cursing Whittington and Anders and pounding with his fists until he was out of breath. But he kept hitting it, on and on, imagining that he was pounding Whittington's big gut. Eventually his arms would hardly move, but he didn't stop. He was down on his knees by then, and his arms were just flailing in front of him. He was covered with sweat, and he was still mumbling the vilest words he knew. But he never cried.

Finally he stopped and sat quietly by his bed. He had told Willard he would come over today. But he couldn't go. He just couldn't do it anymore. It *was* sick. It wasn't normal to hang around with an old man like that. He stayed in his room, not even listening to the radio. After a while he got up and lay down, but he hardly moved until his mother came home. Then he got up and locked the door. But he was scared. He was starting to hear the words again, dripping through his mind like drops from a leaky faucet.

CHAPTER 10

||||||||||||||||||||||||||||||||||||||||||||||||||||||||||||||||||||||||||||

Mark could hear his mother in the kitchen, and then he heard her talking to Ronnie. Before too long she might be checking to see where he was. He didn't want that. He didn't want her to ask how school had been, why he hadn't gone to Willard's, why he was in the bedroom with the door locked—or anything else. He wanted to be alone. And then he was climbing out the window. It was a stupid thing to do, and he would just have to pay for it later, but it was better than talking to her right now.

And once again he was going to Willard's. It didn't

make sense. Someone might see him. Besides, he had just vowed not to go there anymore. But that's where he was going, and he didn't even try to figure himself out.

Willard was downstairs working on the train. "Well, Austin," he said, "I thought maybe you weren't coming."

Mark didn't want Willard's questions either. Especially he didn't want him to mention what the guys on the bus had been yelling. "Well, Gurney," Mark said, "I'll be honest with you. Those kids of mine has been acting up. I had to go down and bail that darn Horace out of jail again."

Willard had been peeling off some old synthetic grass from a little pasture, but now he turned toward Mark. "Are you all right?" he asked.

"Sure. But it ain't too nice when your five-year-old boy has a record as long as his arm—especially when the kid's arms almost touch the ground."

Willard studied Mark's face, as though he was trying to understand what was going on. But finally he said, "What's he in jail for?" But he used his own voice.

"Armed robbery this time. He's been in for all kinds of things—public drunkenness, disturbing the peace—and once for failure to yield the right of way."

Willard picked up his scraper again, and in Gurney's deep voice, he said, "Failure to yield the right of way? You mean to say that little boy drives a car already?"

"No. That's the trouble. He's going to get hisself kill't stopping cars with his bare hands like that."

Old Willard chuckled to himself, and then after a little time to think, he said, "He must be terrible mean, McGill."

"Yuh, he's mean all right. But he ain't so bad as his sister." Mark had thought of all these lines earlier in the day, and now he was running through them, but inside he felt scared, almost panicky. For one thing, he kept remembering where most of these stupid jokes had really come from.

"Oh, yeah? What's so mean about her?"

"Well, she fights a lot."

"What do you mean—she beats up on the kids in the neighborhood?"

"Oh, shoot, no. She couldn't work up a sweat doing that. She's a boxer. She's got a thirty-two and one record. And she's knocked out thirty-three of her opponents." Mark stopped and let that one sink in.

"Now hold on there a minute, McGill. How can she have thirty-three knockouts if she's only won thirty-two fights?"

"Easy. She knocked out that one guy, but then they disqualified her for chewing his ear off after he was already on the canvas."

Willard was falling into the pattern now, doing Gurney's voice naturally, letting Mark come up with the punch lines. "She sounds mean all right. Does she fight full-grown men?"

"Well, not always. Sometimes she fights bears."

Willard seemed at a loss for a comeback, but he laughed and put his hand on Mark's shoulder. "Mc-Gill, you're nuts," he said.

"Shoot, Gurney, I ain't half so crazy as my wife."

"Well, listen, McGill ol' buddy. We better get to work. You're already late. How come you didn't come over after school? Are you feeling okay?" He was still using Gurney's voice.

"Yuh, I'm fine," Mark said, "but my wife's not. They stuck her in the loony bin last week."

"Why was that?" Willard said, but he looked rather serious.

"She thought she was a chicken."

Willard chuckled and shook his head. "Austin, you must be running out of jokes if you're going to do the old one about how we sure can use the eggs."

Mark was a little embarrassed. He *was* running out of jokes. Willard had spoken good-naturedly, but in his own voice. Mark quieted after that. He got a putty knife out of Willard's toolbox and went to work scraping off the old grass on another part of the board. The two worked without saying much for quite a while, and Mark tried just to concentrate on the task at hand, but eventually Willard walked over toward Mark. "Did you notice that I got all these switches in the yard set up now? You can back in and out and pick up cars, just like they really do it in a railroad yard."

Mark came closer and looked at the tracks, and then he stooped and went under the board to the controls.

He started the Union Pacific train up, very slowly. "How do I drop cars off?" he asked.

"Hit that button by your right hand there. And do it as the cars pass over this spot right here. See what I mean?"

Mark pushed the button, and some cars came uncoupled. "I did it too soon," he said. He stopped the train and backed it up, picking up the cars again. This time he uncoupled only the caboose; then he brought the train well forward and stopped it. "Which switch do I throw now to back it in that line with the extra box cars?"

Willard leaned over and pointed to the right switch. Mark moved it over and backed the train into a line with several cars sitting without an engine. The cars coupled, and Mark pulled the whole train ahead. It was much longer now.

"Don't forget your caboose, McGill," Willard said.

"Gurney, I never forget my caboose. You worry about your caboose, and I'll worry about mine." He stopped the train, and then he backed it and threw another switch at the same time. He came back into the line where he had left the caboose, picked it up, and then he took the whole train all the way around the board.

"Where you going, McGill?"

Mark took a moment to answer. He was trying to think of something funny to say. "Kansas City, St. Louis, Washington, New York, London, Paris and Hong Kong. You wanna go?"

"No thanks," Willard said. "The ocean's too bumpy for me."

Mark didn't stop the train at the yard. He kept it going, switching into the far loop, through the upper tunnel. He pushed the little lever on the sound panel that blew the whistle. "You know, Gurney," Mark said, "she's still clicking where she comes out of that tunnel. Maybe we ought to work on that joint I made up there."

"All right, McGill. Why don't you bring the train in and then take a run out there and see if you can repair that line."

"Okay, Gurney. Can you handle things here while I'm gone?"

"Sure. Just don't take so many of the crew with you that I don't have anyone left here in the yard."

"Right. But I'll need three or four good men. We might have to tear out some track and lay that whole bed a little different this time."

"Well, I know. You'll need some help."

Mark pulled the train in and took his crew of men to the far regions of the upper mountain run. It was no easy work detail. He had to call back several times for extra supplies, and Gurney shipped them out on a flat-bed car, powered with a small locomotive. It took a few days, but when the bed was laid again and the track was linked, this time the joint was better. And for at least an hour Mark had thought only of the train, had not remembered school or his mother, not even Larry Whittington.

When Mark came back, he ran the train around the outer loop several times, and the two of them commented on how much smoother the run was now. Then Mark brought the train back around. "Now you be careful coming into the yard, McGill," Willard said. "Don't be causing another train wreck."

"What are you talking about? That last one wasn't my fault. Didn't you hear me yell 'duck'?"

Willard laughed. "I swear you *are* nuts, McGill—or I mean, Austin."

But Mark didn't want him to take on his own voice. He wanted to keep playing—or whatever it was they were doing. And then, suddenly, he felt stupid. He thought of Anders and Whittington. What would they think if they heard him down in this old basement playing trains with an old man? "Well, I guess I better be going now," Mark said.

"Now what's wrong, Austin? You're the most changeable kid I ever met. One minute you're fooling around, and the next one you're looking like you ain't got a friend in the world."

"Nothing's wrong," Mark said. "I just have to go."

"Listen, did you eat before you come over?"

"No."

"Won't your mother be upset? It's past six." Willard pulled his watch from his pocket and snapped it open. "In fact, it's almost six-thirty."

"I don't care."

"But what about your mother? Does she know where you are?"

"She probably does."

"What do you mean 'probably'?"

"Well, this is where I've been going all the time lately."

"I know, Austin, but you shouldn't do that. You should tell her—or else get home in time for supper."

"I know. I just—"

"I don't want your mother getting all upset with me. She must think—"

"All right, Willard," Mark said, his voice suddenly harsh, "I'll go now." He started toward the stairs.

"Austin, hold on a minute."

"My name's Mark."

"All right. Mark." Willard stood still. Mark could see his old hands shaking. "Now listen a minute. You got to quit thinking everyone's your enemy. You got a chip on your shoulder the size of a mountain." Mark stared at him, saying nothing. "And don't give me that look of yours. You don't need to do that to me." But Mark didn't change his look at all. He just wanted to get out of there. "You turn and run if I say the slightest little thing to you that you don't happen to like."

"I've got to go, all right?"

"But why did you do this in the first place, Austin?"

"Do what?"

"Wait so long to come over, and then stay right through suppertime."

"I don't know."

"Did it have anything to do with what those boys

were yelling at me today—about you coming over here?"

"No."

"Are you sure?"

"Yes. Those guys are idiots. I don't care what they say."

"I don't believe that, Austin." Mark shrugged, and again his eyes began to shut Willard out. "I think you have some pretty serious problems. And I think it all has to do with your dad. It still bothers you about him dying, don't it?"

"Look, Willard, I don't want to talk about any of that. I told you that before."

"All right. Go ahead. But you're making a big mistake. If you'd talk about it—to me or to somebody—it might do you some good." Mark felt some of the hardness giving way. He really was tempted to talk to Willard about it. But where could he start? "How did he die anyway, Austin?"

Suddenly the wall closed back in. "I'll see you later, Willard. Maybe I'll come over tomorrow. I'm not sure." He headed up the stairs, but when he got outside he still couldn't face going home. By now Mrs. Pederson had probably called. He would have to answer all kinds of questions before the night was over, but at least he could still put it off for a while longer.

CHAPTER 11

‖‖‖
‖‖‖

Mark went to the arcade and just hung around, watching other people play the electronic games. It wasn't fun, and the time passed slowly, but it was nine-thirty before he finally left for home. He knew his mother was going to have plenty to say, but he had no intention of saying anything. He worked at establishing his shell. Maybe she would ground him for a while, but that was about the worst she would do.

He walked in the door and into the kitchen. His mother was sitting at the kitchen table—with Don. He had not been ready for that.

When his mother looked up, Mark could see that

she had been crying. "Mark, sit down," she said. He had not expected such softness.

He walked over to the table and pulled out a chair. Don and Mother were on opposite sides from each other, near the wall. Mark sat at the end, as far from them as he could get. "Mark, I don't know why you went out the window. And I don't know what's going on." Mark could tell that she was worried, maybe even scared. "When you didn't come home for so long, I went over to Mr. Willard's and he said you had left there. So I called Don, and he came over and we drove around looking for you." She sniffed and then wiped her nose with the tissue she was holding. "We saw you at the arcade. Just standing there like a lost soul. But I didn't want to go in and drag you out. I told Don just to come back here and we'd wait until you decided to come home. But Mark, we're going to talk now; we've got to get to the bottom of this whole thing."

Mark stared at the wall between the two of them. He could see the little yellow and orange flowers set in diamond patterns. He concentrated on that wallpaper and resolved to get through this one, to hold out. "I have a feeling," his mother said, "that this involves Don, and that's why I wanted him to be here. You know that Don and I are getting serious, don't you? Is that bothering you?"

Mark looked at the flowers. He held his face completely still. He tried not even to let his eyelashes move.

"Mark, you can't do this to me tonight. It's your

little game—your defense, or whatever. But I can't take it anymore. You *have* to talk to us."

Mark took a deep breath, let it out slowly, and held his eyes where they had been. He felt sorry for his mother—and he felt sorry for himself. But he didn't want to talk. She would just say the same things all over again. And he could never talk while Don was there anyway.

"Listen," Don said, and he pushed his hand out along the table as though he were thinking of touching Mark. Mark eased back in his chair. "I told you once before that my parents were divorced. I used to hate the men who came around and dated my mother. But I was a kid, younger than you. I've since grown out of that, and now I wish that I had handled things different. My mother's still alone, and she wouldn't have to be. I think she hesitated to remarry because of me—and my sister. It wasn't fair. If I had it to do over again, I wouldn't be that way."

At least he hadn't asked a question. Mark glanced up at the clock. He had an instinct for insulting little symbolic acts of that kind. He even surprised himself at times.

"Mark," his mother said, "I think you can see what Don is saying. We *are* thinking about getting married. We've only been going out for a couple of months, but we've at least talked about it. I feel though that we have to solve this problem first. There's no reason we can't all live together happily. Is there?" Mark didn't move. Several seconds went by. "*Mark*, this is not *fair*. If you don't want us to get married, at least say so. We've just got to talk."

"I don't want to talk, Mom. I've told you that before. We just say the same things over and over."

"But this is something different. You've been closing in tighter and tighter lately. You hardly speak to me at all. I just thought maybe it had to do with Don and me."

"Mom, I don't care whether you marry him or not. It's your own business." He said "him" as though Don were not even in the room.

"But it's your business, too. We would all live together. We'd be a family again, Mark."

"What do you mean, 'again'? We've *never* been a family."

Mom looked down at the table for a time, watching her hands as she twisted the tissue around her fingers. "Mark, I'm not sure what that's supposed to mean. I guess you're referring to the divorce and the troubles before that. But I have *tried*. I've done my best. I can't help it that things went so badly with your dad. I want to make things go better now. But it can't happen unless you come out of this 'thing' you've been in these last few months."

She was wearing a sweat shirt and a pair of jeans. She should have looked sloppy, but she didn't. The jeans and tight shirt only emphasized her figure, and the red scarf tied through her hair accented her blondeness. And she was still made-up—even after worrying all evening, even after crying. It bothered him that she looked that way tonight, bothered him that Don was seeing it, too.

"Mark, would it be better if I left?" Don said.

"I don't care."

"No, Don," Mom said. "I don't think so. Maybe you can help. I haven't been able to do this on my own."

"I know, Lotty. But I'm afraid I'm just mounting the pressure. How can Mark say what he wants to—about *me*—while I'm sitting here? I think I'll run along for tonight. Maybe we can all talk another time."

Mom nodded, releasing him. Mark could feel his own breath coming unsteadily. Why had he called her that? Her name was Charlotte. The only one who had ever called her Lotty was his dad.

Don walked by Mrs. Austin and brushed a little kiss across her cheek, and then he left, telling her not to get up. As soon as the front door closed, she said, "Okay, Mark. We're going to talk. Either that or we'll sit at this table all night—and all day again. But we're going to talk. I have to know what's going on. Your math teacher called tonight and said you don't do your homework. And Mr. Willard said he's worried about you. He said you're happy one minute and angry the next. All I can say is, he sees a side of you I thought was long gone. I haven't seen you happy for months." She sat then for a time, seeming to collect her thoughts. Mark looked up at the clock. It was after ten. He wanted to go to bed. He wanted to sleep.

"All right, Mark. I'm going to ask you some questions. I want answers."

Mark wondered whether his door was still locked from the inside. He thought about taking off for his bedroom and then locking the door behind him.

"Mark, you started to change when your dad left us. And you got a lot worse once he died. Obviously, changing schools hasn't helped either. I have tried and tried to talk to you about all this, but you just deny that any of it has bothered you—except for the school. I'm sorry, but I don't believe you. I think you're holding things back. I want to know how you felt about your dad leaving us."

Mark knew he would have to say something—something to appease her so that she would let him go to bed. "I hated him. I was glad to see him go. You know that."

"And what about me. Didn't you feel I was partly to blame for what happened?"

"No."

"Are you being honest, Mark?"

"Yes."

"Come on now. Try. Please, Mark. What did you think when we used to fight—and when he hit me that time? Did you take his side sometimes? Did you think I deserved it?"

"No." His voice was suddenly intense. "I just hated him. He hit me too—lots of times. And I hated him every time he did it." Mark could feel his stomach quivering. He didn't want to go through this.

"Look, Mark, I know that. You've told me that before. But I'm trying to get past what we've said before. There's something wrong between us. Sometimes I think you hate me, too. Do you feel that I drove your father away?"

"No, Mom. I keep telling you, I was glad when he was gone. He was a big phony. He was a liar. He was always telling me we were going to do all these great things, and we never did any of them." Mark stopped for a moment, tried to calm himself. "He kept saying he wasn't going to drink anymore, too. But he kept doing it—and that's when he was always so . . . you know how he was."

"But Mark, he was good and loving sometimes too. He was weak, and he was mixed-up, and he never did grow up really. But he wanted to do better. He always meant well. Can't you forgive him?"

"No."

"Mark, come on. You loved him so much. I used to watch you when he would come home. You would light up just to see him. Remember how you two used to joke together? He was funny, wasn't he? I mean, really witty. And you used to have so much of that in you. Remember how he used to do all those voices and tell those stupid stories. You loved that, Mark. You loved *him*. I know you did."

"No, Mom, I didn't. I *didn't*. He was funny sometimes, but it was all an act. When he changed—when he would drink—he was so. . . . I hated him, Mom.

I still do." Mark was beginning to panic. This had to stop.

"But why hate him now? What good does that do? Let's just remember what was best about him. Let's let the rest go."

"Mom, what are you talking about? How can you just forget the things he did to you? He called you filthy names. He accused you of all kinds of awful things. Remember that morning he tore your blouse and screamed at you for dressing up when you went to work? Remember what he called you?" Mark stopped and took a long breath. "Do you remember what he said about you and your boss?"

"Mark, all right. Yes, I remember. But I also remember how sorry he was after. He didn't mean it. He just had such a stupid temper when he was drinking."

"But that's not enough, Mom. You can't hurt someone that much and then just cry and say you're sorry the next day. That's what he *always* did. He always wanted to hug me after he had hit me. He would come into my bedroom, smelling like whiskey, and would try to kiss me. And then he'd cry if I wouldn't let him."

"But Mark, there's a lot more to it. He had so many things working against him. His own dad made things so tough for him. He could never do enough to be as great as his father. There were just lots of things going on in your dad. He was a big athlete in high school; and when he didn't make it in college, he dropped out completely. He couldn't handle it. But, Mark, we all have things to go through. Your dad didn't deal with his problems very well, but . . . well, look at yourself, honey. You're having a rough time yourself. You need to think of it that way; you need to forgive him, Mark. We just have to do that. It isn't easy for me to forget either, you know."

Mark felt something. He felt something give way a little. And suddenly he wanted to feel more. He wanted some things to be over with. He was even trying to think of something to say—both to his mother and to himself.

"Mark, do you think it especially bothers you that your dad died the way he did?"

Mark was stunned. He had never thought she would say anything about that. "Why should that matter?" He tried to sound calm.

"What caused his death, Mark?"

"He was drunk. He drove off the road."

"No, he wasn't, Mark. You know that. He had been drinking earlier, when he came to talk to us, but when—"

"I don't want to do this, Mom. I don't like to think about that day."

"You've got to, Mark. You know what happened."

"It was an accident, Mom." Mark stood up. He was shaking.

"No, it wasn't. You know it wasn't, Mark. You and I are the only two who *do* know."

"No, Mom. Don't say that. Come on."

"Mark, you know what he said to us. And he had said it lots of times before. He described exactly how

116

he was going to do it—even where he would—"

"Mom, *no.*" Mark backed toward his room. "Listen, I know what you mean. I haven't forgotten about that. I know exactly what you mean. But he wouldn't have done it. I just know he wouldn't."

Mark had reached his door. "Honey, don't run now. Come on. We have to get this out. It's not our fault. I know how he stood there and cried, but he had done it so many times before. I had no choice, Mark. Neither did you. I know what we said was hard for him to hear, but what else could we say?"

"Mom, I don't remember what I said. I don't know what you mean. He was drunk, and he drove off the road. That's all. Honest. I think you're the one who needs to forget all this."

"Mark, stay here. Let's get this out in the open."

"No. I need some sleep." He tried the door and found that it was unlocked.

"Mark, please."

"No. Not now. I can't." Mark went in and shut the door, locking it behind him. He lay down on his bed without taking his clothes off, shaking all over. All right, maybe he knew. But that didn't mean they had to talk about it. And she had no right to force him. She was the one who had refused to say anything about it at first. What was she trying to do now?

He could hear her crying. She was close to the door, sobbing. Mark wanted to cry too, but it was important that he not do it. That would be letting go. He had to hold all of this out—not let it in.

CHAPTER 12

||||||||||||||||||||||||||||||||||||||||||||||||||||||||||||||

Mark slept late the next morning, since it was Saturday. Each time he woke up, he forced himself not to think and to slip back into the emptiness of sleep. But that only worked so long. At about nine-thirty he gave up and got out of bed. His mind had started to return to the conversation of the night before, but he didn't want to think about those things.

Mom was sitting in the kitchen with her robe on, having a cup of coffee. Ronnie was eating a bowl of cereal, sitting across the table. Mark was scared that Mom would want to start where she had left off the night before, so he walked straight to the bathroom and then went back to his room and finished dressing. When he came out, he told his mother he had promised Mr. Willard that he would help him that morning —which, of course, was a lie. She made him eat a couple slices of toast before he left, but she didn't push him to talk.

Willard was already working on the layout. He had replaced the old grass with some very realistic looking stuff that sprinkled on, and he was gluing down some little figures of cows and sheep. "Well, good morning, Austin. I thought maybe you wouldn't come back today."

"I thought I might as well," Mark said, but he didn't feel much like talking.

Willard seemed to recognize that, or maybe he didn't feel like talking himself. He looked tired. "Maybe we can fix up that one set of hills that are broke down, if you can stick around for a while."

"All right," Mark said. He wished that he could think of something for McGill to say. That would be the easiest. Then they could move into the other voices and not have to face each other. But he didn't seem to have it in him this morning. And so they worked without really talking much, except when Willard gave instructions as Mark did the replastering. It was a fairly simple process of dipping paper towels in plaster and building up some hills that had fallen in. But the shaping took a certain amount of skill. Willard was obviously pleased at how well Mark picked up the knack of it.

When they finished the project, it was almost noon. Willard said he needed to sit down and rest for a while. "Do you want some lunch?" he asked. "We can fix a bowl of soup. I feel like I need something."

"Yuh, that's all right. I want to run this for a minute though, okay?"

Mark ran one of the trains around the big loop. And he started up the little coal train. "You know, Willard, we could add to the board over that way from the roundhouse—there's room there to add three or four feet—and then we could put in another loop out that direction."

"I know. I've thought about that. I even thought about putting in quite a high mountain and then running a little tram up it."

"Yuh. That'd be good. Do you want to do it?"

"Well, let's get everything else fixed up first, and then maybe we could think about that." Willard actually sounded less than enthusiastic, however.

"What are you going to do when you get this all fixed-up, Willard? Play trains all day?"

Willard chuckled. "I might as well. I guess I'm in my second childhood anyway. I'm just a senile old man."

"What am I? A senile kid?"

"I don't know what you are, Austin. I've been trying to figure that out. You know, your mom told me last night that you haven't been doing your schoolwork, and that you—"

"Come on, Willard. That's not your problem—

that's mine." He said it fairly politely, not with hostility, but Willard silenced immediately. "Hey, Gurney," Mark said, suddenly assuming McGill's voice. "Did I tell you my wife had a baby yesterday?"

Willard didn't answer. He just looked at Mark across the board.

"Yuh, in fact, she had twins," Mark said. "But the two of them don't look much alike." Mark waited again, but he got no response. "They're both a little strange, but I guess they average out all right. See, the one only has one eye, but the other one has three, so it works out just fine." Mark waited. It was another one of the stupid things his dad used to say. Maybe it wasn't all that funny, but he wanted Willard to come back with Gurney's booming voice. He didn't. "And the one has. . . ." Mark stopped. He couldn't think of anything else to say. He looked down at the trains in front of him. "What's the matter, Willard?"

"You're the one who needs to answer that question, Austin."

Mark decided he might as well leave. He was trying to think of something to use as an excuse. But then Willard said, "Listen, Austin, why don't we have that lunch? I'm not feeling so good. I guess I been on my feet too long. Do you suppose you could heat up a can of soup for us?"

"Yuh. Sure."

Willard climbed the stairs very slowly, clinging to the rail, and his breath came with difficulty. He stopped and waited a couple of times, coughing again.

"Have you caught cold or something?" Mark asked.

"Naw. I got something worse than that. It's called seventy-nine, going on eighty."

Willard sat down at the old pine kitchen table and told Mark where he could find a can of soup and where the can opener was. Mark got out a pan and mixed the water into the soup as it heated. It was something he had done every day the summer before when he was out of school and his mother was at work. The very act reminded him of those awful days when he had had to look out for Ronnie and couldn't go anywhere, and when he had had all day to think. His dad had died in May. It had been a very long summer.

"Well, Gurney," Mark said, in his McGill voice. "You eat a little soup, and you'll feel like a million bucks. Of course, a million ain't what it used to be."

Willard nodded, but he spoke in his own voice. "That's for sure. I'm down to about a dollar and a half."

"Are you really feeling that lousy, Willard?"

Willard didn't answer. He blew on his chicken noodle soup. "There's some crackers in the cupboard," he said. "The one in the middle. Would you mind grabbing them for us?"

Mark got up and found the crackers. They were saltines in a black and white "no name" box. "But are you all right, Willard?"

"Well, no. I'm not. But I guess I'm not doing too bad either. Most of my friends are already dead."

Mark didn't like chicken noodle soup. He toyed

with it more than he ate it, but he ate some crackers. "Willard, do you think about death a lot? I mean— you know—when you see your friends dying."

" 'Course I do."

"Does it scare you?"

"Well, I don't know. I guess death don't scare me too much anymore. But dying still does." He chuckled to himself.

"Sometimes would you—" Mark stopped. Maybe he shouldn't ask it.

"What?"

"Well, sometimes do you think you'd like to just have it over with?"

Willard laughed again. "I don't know, Austin. I guess sometimes I do feel that way. But I cling to life, too. I don't get very excited about jumping into something I can't get out of if it turns out I don't like it." He lifted a spoonful of soup, blew on it, his cheeks puffing out, and then he gulped it down.

There was something else Mark wanted to know, but he didn't know how to ask it. In a way, it seemed that maybe he had thought more about death than Willard had.

"You better down that soup, boy," Willard said. "I feel better already now that I got something in me."

Mark spooned in a mouthful. "I guess we better quit for today," he said. "You better rest this afternoon. Maybe there's a football game on TV you can watch."

"I guess maybe you're right." He pushed the bowl

away and set his elbows on the table. Mark looked at his old bony hands, all spotted and brown. "That's the trouble with being old, Austin. You see the things you want to do, but you can't do 'em. You start out on something with a lot of energy and all, and then it's gone before you know it. You feel like you're getting cheated all the time, like someone keeps putting something nice in front of you and then pulling it back just when you reach for it."

"But you usually seem happy, Willard."

"Well, I'll tell you, Austin. I usually don't think too much and just sort of take the days as they come. That's the best way. But when I do think about it, it don't make me feel too good to know that two weeks after I'm dead there ain't going to be one person who'll remember me. My own kids won't even care."

There were things Mark wanted to say, things he thought he ought to say. But he couldn't do it. He looked at Willard, but not into his eyes.

"I'll tell you something, Austin. The only thing I ever done in my life that was a little more than just making a living was build that little train layout down there. Ain't that a sorry thing to say at the end of your life?" Willard picked up a little paper package of saltines and tore it open. He had some difficulty getting hold of a cracker to pull out, however. Mark wanted to help him, but he was too embarrassed to do it. "What are you going to do with your life, Austin?"

Mark had known this was coming, and he didn't

want to talk about it. "I think that train's a pretty good accomplishment," he said.

Willard looked up, smiling a little. "Well, I appreciate that, Austin. And I appreciate your help. But answer the question."

"I don't know, Willard. I don't know what I want to do. I'm not very good at anything."

"You little fool," Willard said. His voice sounded sad more than angry. "You're smart—ten times smarter than I ever was. You can pick up something and understand it in a second. You're a good reader too—and I never was. It don't make sense to sit around and talk that way about yourself."

"Willard, I told you before, I don't want to talk—"

"That's right. You don't want to talk about anything that might get you thinking about what you're doing to yourself." Now Willard sounded irritated, impatient.

"It's not your business, Willard." Mark knew he was getting angry, but his voice was still under control.

"Don't tell me that," Willard said. "I don't deserve that. We're friends." Mark was edging out of his seat. He didn't know what to say, but he was going to leave. "Look, Austin—*Mark*—I don't mean to climb all over you. I hated that when I was a kid too. But I just can't understand why you don't even bother to do your homework. You have the ability to do it so—"

"I hate school, Willard. I hate the kids, and I hate the teachers. I hate everything about that place. When I get out of there, all I want to do is forget it."

"But that's stupid. Can't you see that?"

"Maybe it is. But the school is stupid, too."

"And who's going to lose? The school can't lose."

"I just want to get away from that place."

"Sure, and then you'll hate the high school, and after that you'll hate your job—so you'll quit that and hate something else. You've chosen hate, Austin. And that ain't something you *have* to do."

"You'd hate that place too, Willard. You've heard how those guys act."

"Kids at that age do stupid things, Austin. But you don't have to ruin your life because of it." Willard was breathing hard now; he started to cough.

"Look, Willard. I like to come over here—because of the trains and. . . . But if you're going to start in on me, just like my mom and everyone else, I'm not coming anymore."

"Well, Austin, maybe you shouldn't come then. Because if you do, I'm likely to start telling you the same thing all over again. It's what you need to hear. Your mother says it all started when your dad died, and I can understand that—but listen, you ain't the first kid who ever had a father die. You can't spend the rest of your life just—"

"Leave me alone," Mark said, sharply, almost viciously. He stood up. "I don't have to listen to this," he said, and he headed for the door.

"Wait a minute, Austin," Willard said, but only as Mark was shutting the door behind him.

CHAPTER 13

Mark wandered down to the arcade for a while, but he had no money. The place only made him nervous when he couldn't play. So he went home, went to his bedroom and shut the door; but all he could do there was sit on his bed and stare at the wall. He was tired, and he was empty. And when he finally flopped back on his bed, he fell asleep. He slept for almost two hours. As he woke up, eventually, he could hear Don out in the kitchen. The guy was around the place more all the time now.

Mark put his hands behind his head and stared at the ceiling. There was not one thing he wanted to do.

He hated television, and he hated to read. Every plot seemed to be about some little problem that got solved in an hour or in a couple hundred pages. He was hungry, but he didn't want to go out and have to talk to his mother and Don. Actually, what he wanted to do was work on the train. Maybe he could apologize to Willard and then just go down the basement and not talk. But Willard wouldn't let him get away with that anymore. He just wanted to push—like everyone else.

Why did everyone think he was so stupid? They all kept telling him he was ruining his life—as though that were some brilliant insight. Did they really think he didn't know that? Who knew better than he did how unhappy he was? Did they think he didn't want to "do something" with his life? But it wasn't that easy. There were things they didn't know about, and those things didn't just go away. He couldn't just push them out of his mind. He had been trying—really trying—for a long time, and it didn't work.

No one knew what had been jabbing away at him—except Mom. And she didn't know it all. She hadn't been there at the very last. She could forget—she had Don now. But it wasn't that easy for him.

He was beginning to feel the old panic again. The words hadn't come into his head yet, but they would. They were hovering behind his consciousness, waiting to start throbbing at the edges, and then to push their way into the front of his head. He did not want to hear it all again. Not the conversation. Not the last words. Mark rolled over and switched on the radio. The news was on. He switched it back off and jumped up. There had to be something better.

He walked to the door and swung it open. "Mom," he said. She turned toward him from where she was standing near the kitchen cabinet. Don was next to her, cutting carrots into sticks. "Mom, could I have a couple of bucks?"

"Yuh, I guess so. Why?"

"Could I just have it?"

"Come on, Mark. You know I don't just—"

"All right. I want to go to the arcade. I want to play Space Invaders. I want to waste the whole thing on a stupid electronic game." Don laughed at Mark's irony, but Mom didn't.

"All right, Mark. I know you like to play those games. You can go down for a while. But we'll be having dinner in about five minutes. You can go right after that. But I need you back here by eight—well, let's say eight-thirty. Don and I wanted to go to a movie. We can go to one that starts at nine, but someone will have to be here with Ronnie."

Mark wanted to protest. He wanted to go now. He wanted to run all the way. But he couldn't say that to her. She didn't know about the words that were trying to get into his head again, and he couldn't tell her. So he would have to sit down and eat, or she wouldn't let him go. "Okay," he said, and he even tried to sound normal.

"Wash up then. And help me set the table. Or

better yet, go out and see if you can hunt Ronnie down."

Mark walked outside and called for Ronnie. When he got no answer, he walked down the street, looking and occasionally calling. He found Ronnie at a neighbor's house and told him to head for home. All the while, he was saying to himself that he could hang on for a little longer. At least he was going to get some money and he wouldn't have to spend the whole evening at home.

Don and Mother talked about the usual sort of news and weather at the dinner table. Don worked for the telephone company, in the main office, and he had some stories to tell about dumb complaints and requests he had gotten lately. Mark ate quickly, downing the casserole his mother had fixed and drinking lots of milk. Ronnie was eating with his mouth open, which Mark could hardly tolerate, but he didn't say anything to the little jerk, and he ignored Don.

"Okay, I'm going now. I'll be back by eight, or eight-thirty at the latest. Could I have the money?"

"Where's he going?" Ronnie asked.

"None of your business," Mark said, not loudly but with hostility.

Mrs. Austin had gotten up and was looking in her purse. "Now, don't start that," she said, "or you won't be going at all."

All right. All right. He just wanted the money and the chance to get out the door. "Don, honey, all I have is a ten. Do you have a couple of ones you could give him?"

Don't call him that. For crying out loud, Mom. How can you do that?

Don stood up and got his wallet out of his back pocket. He turned toward Mark, so that Mother couldn't see, and he slipped over three dollars instead of two. Mark wanted to throw one of them—all three of them—back in his face. But he said, "Thanks a lot," and then he walked out the door. As soon as he was outside, he began to run. It was six blocks to the arcade, and he ran all the way, not hard, but steadily and efficiently. He didn't want to get so tired that he would have to stop and walk.

When he got there, people were playing both of the Space Invaders games. After a few minutes of watching, he could see that both guys were pretty good and would be a while. So he got change from the man up front and spent a couple of quarters playing Asteroids. But he wasn't very good at that, and he knew he would blow his money fast if he kept playing. Better just to watch awhile. He walked down and studied the guys who were playing Space Invaders. The little figures marched in across the screen to the rippling sounds of electronic music. In a second or so the beat of the attack began, and the twanging sound of shooting. The little creatures began popping on the screen, making bursting noises, but others kept coming, moving down, shifting back and forth, shooting, waving their little arms, and gradually coming faster. But the kid playing was good. He cleared the whole board and laughed, a dumb sort of giggle of satisfaction, and then he waited as the figures moved in across the screen again.

The kid glanced up at Mark. He was fairly big and somewhat older than Mark, yet he seemed to want praise; but Mark was only hoping that he would get hit again—soon. He had used up two of his bases and only had one to go. Mark really needed to get his hands on that machine.

But it was another ten minutes or so before the guy finally got hit. As soon as he did, Mark said, "Could I play once before you play again?" Mark had done this before, and it usually worked. Once he got on and guys saw how good he was—how long he could stay alive—they would wander off to other games.

"Okay," the kid said, after a hesitation. "You any good?"

Mark waited until he had dropped the money in, and then he said, "Better than you'll ever be."

"Hey, shorty, don't talk so tough. I didn't have to give you that thing, you know." But Mark was watching the screen fill up with little invaders. When they began to come at him, Mark eliminated them, quickly, precisely, systematically. The other guy waited long enough to see that Mark's boast was correct, and then he walked away without saying anything.

Mark gave himself over to the game. The grimy room and all the noise of the machines and the people, the whole world, slipped away for the moment. Mark cleared the board over and over, almost never missing, taking the little creatures off in exactly the same pattern each time. But that was the problem. Once he got into the swing of things, the game was too easy. It was almost a habit, automatic, and there was room for thought. The image of Don back in the kitchen with Mom kept coming to mind. And the thought kept returning that after a little while he would have to go back and sit in the house the rest of the evening—with nothing to do, nothing to fill his head. He wished he could go somewhere else, do something. This stupid game was not enough.

What was Willard doing? How angry was he? Mark wanted to go there. But he couldn't do that. Willard would want to talk. Suddenly Mark turned away from the machine. He was in the middle of an attack, had only cleared half the screen.

"Are you finished?" someone said.

"What?"

"Are you finished?"

"No." He looked at the screen. He had been hit, his base wiped out. But he still had two more to go. "Yes," he said, and he walked away.

"Hey, you still have two more turns," the kid said.

Mark walked to the front of the place, past the machines and the noise. A girl, jumping up and down and squealing, bumped into Mark. But Mark slipped by and went on outside. He stood on the sidewalk and looked around him. It was dark and there was no-where to go.

Suddenly he turned and went back, directly to the game he had just walked away from. "Hey, I have two more bases."

"Not now. You only have one. I just lost one for you." He was a pleasant-faced kid with blond hair; he grinned and stepped away. "Take it now. Hurry." Mark stepped up and started to move and shoot im-mediately. "You're sure good," the kid said. "A lot better than me."

Mark kept the game going a long time. When he finally lost his last base, he didn't even notice what his score was; he just dropped his money in again and started over. And he did the same again after that game. He played until twenty minutes after eight, and then he just walked away from a game without finish-ing it. He really didn't care. He was bored by it any-way.

He ran all the way home. His mother and Don were waiting, ready to go. As soon as they left, Mark sat down in front of the television set, across from Ronnie. But the show was dumb, and in a few minutes he couldn't stand to sit there any longer. He got up and went to his room where he turned on the radio, loud, but he knew that nothing would hold it all back any longer. So he just let the whole scene pass through his mind. It was almost easier not to fight it. "I don't be-lieve you," he was saying, and his dad was crying. And then he was saying the last words, the ones Mom hadn't heard. And Dad was getting in his car with that look on his face. It had all happened, and it couldn't be erased.

"I hate him," Mark said out loud. "He did it to get back at me."

CHAPTER 14

Mark put in a very difficult week. On Sunday afternoon he spent the last of the money that Don had given him. That meant he had nothing to do all week. School was sort of preoccupying, if unpleasant, but the evenings were long and threatening. And Mark was having more trouble sleeping all the time. The words kept coming into his mind, and he would wake up shaking and sweating. He didn't think much about what the words meant anymore—he simply lived in terror of the repetition. He had always hoped that they would gradually go away, but now he could see that this was not going to happen. He had no idea of what to do. He couldn't talk to a school counselor, because that would mean saying things he didn't want to say. And he couldn't talk to his mother; she already knew too much. Anyway, what he wanted most was simply not to have to talk at all. He just wanted everything to go away. It would be best if he could go to sleep and stay asleep for a very long time.

Mark survived the next Friday and Saturday evenings by getting money from his mother again. He played Space Invaders until the pounding rhythm of the attack was itself like the words that came in the night. But playing the game was still better than doing nothing.

On Sunday morning Mother came into Mark's room and sat down on his bed. "Mark," she whispered.

Mark had been awake, but he pretended not to be. He hoped she would go away. She spoke his name again, however. "What?" he said, with the coldness he had come to use with her most of the time.

"I need to tell you something. Turn over and look at me." Mark didn't move at first, but she tugged softly at his shoulder, and he responded. He turned over and then looked up, his eyes half-open. "Last night Don and I decided that we *do* want to get married. We're not exactly sure when—I guess, to some degree, that's up to you. But we won't want to wait *too* long."

What was that supposed to mean? And why did she have makeup on already on Sunday morning?

"Mark, we want you to feel good about this. I'm not saying you have to jump for joy. These things take time. But we want you to get to know Don better—gradually. I *know* you'll like him."

"Look, Mom, I don't care."

"What do you mean?"

"I mean, I don't care whether you get married or not. It doesn't matter to me."

"That's not exactly your blessing, Mark."

Mark took a breath and rather dramatically blew it out, a signal of his disgust. "Look, Mom, I don't know what you want. You can do whatever you want to—I'm not the one to decide."

"But you don't like Don, do you?"

"Mom, come on. He's Prince Charming. He's Robert Redford and Paul Newman rolled into one. He's Superman. He's—"

"Mark, you're not funny." Mark let his eyes go shut again. "Oh, Mark," his mother said, and sighed. "I try so hard with you. I think about what I want to say, and then I come in here and try to say it just right, but anything I say to you is wrong. I just don't know what to do."

"Get married, Mom. Marry Don or anyone you want to marry. You don't need my permission."

"Mark, what are you talking about? We all have to live together. You can make life miserable for me—*and* for him—if you want to. And I think you want to."

"Then dump me off, Mom. There must be institutions for problem kids like me."

Mark opened his eyes to see tears moving down his

mother's cheeks. For a moment he almost said he was sorry. But instead he rolled over onto his side so he couldn't see her. "Okay, listen," his mother said. "I've blown this, as usual. What I *am* asking you is that you try to get to know Don a little better. He wondered if you wanted to go with him to the Broncos game next Sunday. I remember that you used to ask your dad to take you, and he never got around to it. Don likes football and—"

"I don't."

She hesitated and took a breath of her own. "All right. It doesn't have to be a game. Will you do something with him sometime? Maybe this week. Will you give him a chance?"

"Mom, did you know Don before you and dad got divorced?"

There was silence for a moment, and then his mother stood up. Mark felt the weight lift from the bed. "What?" Mark didn't answer. "Mark, what is that supposed to mean?"

"Nothing."

"Mark, we both know—" She stopped, but Mark could hear her breathing. He knew he should take it back—he knew how wrong it was. "We both know what you mean, don't we, Mark? You nasty little. . . ." Her voice lost control. "All right, Mark. When you run out of your own little games, play the ones your dad taught you. You had a great teacher."

Mark couldn't believe he had done it. He had

wanted to hurt her. But why? He hated himself beyond belief. He forced his face into the pillow and wished he could smother himself.

"Mark, I feel sorry for you," she said, her voice still taut. "I'm sorry that you have let this thing make you so bitter. But I didn't deserve that, and you know it. I thought all that sort of thing was gone from my life. I think you owe me an apology."

She waited. Mark had almost brought himself to say something, just before she had asked. But now he couldn't. She left, shutting the door firmly. Mark flipped over and forced the pillow down over his face, hard. He held on and held on, pushing and straining to keep it down. Maybe some adrenaline would help him push even after he . . . but of course he couldn't do it. He let up gradually. Then he lay on his back, breathing hard from the strain, hating himself as he never had before.

After a time he got up, got dressed, and left. His mother wasn't in the kitchen, and he had no idea of where she was. But that didn't matter. Mark had decided to see Willard. He didn't know what good that would do, but it was what he wanted.

He stepped inside Willard's front door and called out. No one answered. He walked through to the kitchen and called Willard's name again. But the answer came from a room off the kitchen, not from downstairs.

Mark opened the door and looked in. Willard was

in bed, his head propped up with two pillows, but his face looked much whiter than usual. "Are you sick, Willard?" Mark asked.

"Yes. I guess you could call it that."

"What's the matter?"

Willard pointed to a chair by the wall, close to the bed. "Sit down," he said. "Where've you been?"

"I don't know. Just school."

"I got some more work done on the train. I sure could've used you."

"You told me not to come anymore."

"I know. But I didn't think you'd listen to me." Willard chuckled, and then he began to cough.

"What's the matter, Willard? Have you seen a doctor?"

"Oh, sure. I've seen plenty of doctors. I'm going into the hospital in the morning."

"Why?"

"My doctor wants to run some tests. You know, poke a lot of holes in me and take what little blood I've got. That's how the man makes a living. A guy can't keep his doctor from making a livelihood, you know." He had gradually taken on Gurney's voice. "Right, McGill?"

"I know what you mean," Mark said, in his high voice. "My wife is in the hospital again. She's having another baby."

"Is that so?" How many do you have now?"

Mark tried to think of an answer. He wanted to say something funny—really funny. But nothing came.

"Quite a few," he said, lamely, and in his own voice.

Mark watched Willard. His eyes didn't look good. They were faded and yellow. "Listen, Austin," Willard said, with less voice than usual. "I want to talk to you about a couple of things. I was starting to think you weren't coming back." He hesitated after that, as though he were unsure what he wanted to say next. "I won't preach at you anymore, Austin. I messed up my own life, and you have the right to do the same, if that's what you want. It don't do any good anyway. A fellow has to find his own way and make his own mistakes. There ain't no kid in history who ever listened to an old man, so I don't know why I should expect you to be the first one."

Willard's eyes went shut for a moment. "Could you reach up here and push them pillows down under my shoulders a little more, Austin? They're about to break my neck."

Mark stood up and when Willard raised up a little he shoved the pillows down. "Is that okay?"

"Sure. That's fine. So anyway, there's something else. I was thinking I'd like to give you that train layout."

"What?" Mark was suddenly frightened.

"Well, Austin, what's the point of a old man having a toy train? I would like someone to have it who would appreciate it. My kids don't want it, that's for sure."

"What are you talking about, Willard? You just put all that time into fixing it up."

"I know that. I—"

"We'd have to tear it all apart. And I don't have a big enough place for it anyway."

"Well, I know. I thought about that. What I thought I could do was give you the whole house."

Mark couldn't believe what he was hearing—and he didn't like it. "Willard, I don't even know what you're talking about. You can't give me your house."

"Yes. Yes, I can. I've thought about it. I could give you the house, and you and your mother and little brother could move in here. The place is old and needs some fixing up, but I have about six thousand dollars in the bank. And you could use that to fix it up some. It's all paid for. You wouldn't have to put out a dime on house payments. That would help your mother, I think. I need to check with a lawyer and find out exactly what I have to do to—"

"Willard." Mark stood up. "What are you talking about? *You* live here."

Willard's eyes went shut again, slowly, and this time they stayed shut. "Austin, you know what I mean."

"No, I don't."

"Austin, now listen. I'm old. It's nothing more than you must have expected. You knew I was—"

"Willard, I don't understand. I don't. Don't talk like that."

"Austin, I have cancer."

Mark stood by the bed, looking down at the old man's bent brown hands on the top of the bedspread. He hated this man. "When did you find out?" he said, and the anger raged in his voice.

"Well, I—"

"You knew, didn't you? You knew when you came down there when I was shooting baskets. You've known the whole time, haven't you?" But Willard kept his eyes shut and didn't answer. "You *knew*, didn't you?"

"Yes."

"You worthless . . . you. . . ." But Mark could find no words.

"Austin, I want you to have my train." The words came slowly, strained, but with resolution.

"That's all you ever wanted. You keep your stupid train, Willard. It means nothing to me. It's a stupid toy, and you've wasted all this time working on it. I don't care one bit about the stupid thing."

"That's not true," Willard said, but he said it to Mark's back. Mark was getting out. He wanted to run. He wanted to break something. He wanted to hurt someone.

CHAPTER 15

I felt good to be angry. It was an emotion to fill him up for a while. But it didn't last long enough. Mark began walking, without any place to go, and soon the sense of emptiness returned. He had no more options; he could think of absolutely nothing that would help him now. He ended up at the arcade, but he didn't go in. He went right to the door, but the sound of the machines, burping and pinging, unnerved him, and he turned and walked down the street. The wind was picking up, and clouds were moving in. Leaves were blowing around in the streets and on the sidewalk.

Mark ended up in a park, a little playground really, where he sat on a bench for at least an hour, his bare arms held close in against the cold. Almost no one was around. He watched two little boys playing on the swings, all bundled up in winter coats. But he saw them only abstractly, hardly conscious of them. What he wanted to do was think; he wanted to deal with his problem, find some way out. There was no place to run anymore. But no thoughts would come, no organized ideas.

When rain began to fall, he walked home, never running no matter how cold or wet he got. His mother wasn't there. Neither was Ronnie. There was a note on the kitchen table, but Mark didn't read it. He went into his room, lay on his bed and stared at the ceiling, looking at the old-fashioned light fixture and the cobweb in the high corner. He still couldn't think. Because he was cold, he dropped his clothes on the floor and rolled under the covers. It was not yet even dark, but he fell asleep, and he didn't wake up until almost midnight. The rest of the night was agony. He tossed around in his bed and drifted in and out of half-awake dreams. Sometimes he saw Willard, all white and with eyes shut, saying, "I want you to have my train." And sometimes he dreamed he was breaking the train layout, throwing the trains around and smashing the hills and little buildings. And other times it was his dad who was in the bed, replacing Willard, and Mark was crying and saying that he was sorry. By morning Mark felt shaky, disoriented, and terribly tired.

But he got up and dressed and went to school. He didn't speak to anyone, not to his mother, not to his teachers, not to anyone at school. He felt numb, not in touch with what was going on around him. He kept trying to think about Willard, trying to hate him. He wanted to feel something, know something. But Willard was sort of cancelled—with everything else. The words did not come into Mark's head, but he almost would have welcomed them. They had to be better than this blankness.

In math Mrs. Pederson called him up to her desk. She asked him where his homework was, reminded him that he had promised to do it. "You promised me, and you promised your mother," she said. Mark stared at her. Though he heard what she was saying, he couldn't concentrate on what it meant. He was inside his body, and she was looking in at him, peering through the holes of his eyes. He didn't think to answer. It didn't occur to him that it was necessary.

"Are you on drugs?" she said.

Inside, Mark smiled, but the face of his body didn't seem to move. Where would he get drugs? She was out there on the other side of his face, looking, and then her own face began to distort. He thought he was falling for a moment, and he reached out and touched the desk, but it was still suspended in front of him as it had been.

"I'll have to talk to you later, Mark, but now I'm going to write out a blue slip for you. I want you to go down to see a counselor."

She pushed a blue piece of paper toward him. Mark looked at it. When he didn't pick it up, she held it in front of him. Mark wondered what it was for. "Mark, take this. I want you to go *now*."

Mark tried to think what she wanted. He heard laughter somewhere and turned his head in a sweep, the walls gliding by. There were more faces. And he knew them. He had seen these faces before.

And then he was waiting for the bus; something strange had happened. He couldn't remember what he had done all afternoon. This wasn't funny. He didn't like it at all. The bus was there, and guys were pushing to get on, and a girl said to him, "Are you okay?"

"I'm not sure," he said. "I don't like it when time skips like that."

She looked puzzled. Mark knew her face from somewhere. "Are you sick?" she asked.

"No." He got on the bus. The only seat was the wide one at the very back. Mark saw the empty green plastic, and he worked his way toward it. That was a simple matter. He understood exactly what he was doing now. He would go to the plastic and sit down. But there were people all around him, on both sides of the long hallway that led to the back of the bus. And he could not move well, his legs only moving with great effort. People were saying words to him, but he would protect himself—he would keep it all out of his head.

He was sitting finally, smelling the plastic and diesel and the people. And then time skipped again, and a big round-faced boy was standing in the middle of the bus, yelling something. Words. He was saying Mark's name, forcing words into Mark's head. "Austin, do you want to get off here, at your old buddy's house?"

Mark wanted to get rid of the round face, and the words. He was up, suddenly, and he was moving toward the boy. He grabbed for the face, but it moved, and then his own face was against the boy's soft chest, and Mark was struggling to get free, to breathe. He broke loose and came back a step, and then he saw the face clearly, lunged for it. He was trying to tear it away. But someone had hold of him, pulling him backwards, and the face was getting away, but he had some of it in his fingernails.

Mark woke up in bed; he woke slowly, drifting into semi-consciousness many times before he was aware of what was around him. But finally he realized he was in a strange place, a room with other beds. He stared around the room and saw a woman in white, a nurse, coming toward him. A man somewhere in the room was saying, "You can't take it from me. You can't take it from me." The man had been saying those same words for some time now, but Mark had been hearing it only vaguely, as though from a great distance.

"Hello, Mark," the nurse said. "Do you remember where you are?"

"What?"

"Do you know you're in the hospital?"

Mark stared at her. She seemed familiar. He remembered a smiling woman had been standing over his bed once, with a white cap and round glasses. "Did I get hurt?" Mark asked.

"No. You're fine. You got very upset."

Mark looked around him. There was a man in the bed next to him; he was lying flat, staring up at the ceiling, his eyes wide and unblinking. And farther on down the room was the heavy-faced man who was still saying, "You can't take it from me." But he wasn't saying it to anyone, just sitting on his bed, grasping his hands to his chest. "What is this?" Mark said.

"Mark, you got very upset on the school bus. Do you remember that?" Mark remembered the face, the round face. It was Whittington's. He nodded, and then he glanced back at the men in the other beds. "The doctor gave you a rather heavy sedative, and you've been sleeping since you came in yesterday. It's a chance for you to rest and calm down."

Mark felt strange. There were so many things he couldn't remember clearly. Panic welled up in him again. "Where's my mother?"

"She's right outside. She's been waiting for you to wake up. Do you feel like seeing her?"

"Yes." But Mark could feel his breath catching in his chest. He was scared.

"All right. The doctor told me you might be a little concerned when you woke up. He said it would be good for you to see your mother if you felt up to it. Do you think you could get up and walk out to the day room?"

"Yes." There was something about her voice—so practiced, so under control—that made Mark very nervous.

"All right. Your mother brought your robe. I'll help you put it on. You might be dizzy for a time, so I want you to sit up for a minute or two first. And while you're sitting, I'll bring you a glass of orange juice. Then a little later, we'll get you some breakfast. Do you think you can sit up for me now?"

Mark sat up and realized for the first time what a flimsy gown they had put on him. He tried to pull it down over his knees, but it wouldn't reach. The man in the next bed was still staring at the ceiling. Suddenly, Mark wanted to go home. "I'm okay," he said to the nurse. "I don't need to stay here."

She smiled, a confident, warm, fake smile. She was a curly-haired woman with fat cheeks. Mark didn't like her. "I'm sure you're fine, Mark. But you need some rest. And you'll have a chance to talk to the doctor today, or maybe tomorrow. As soon as you feel up to it."

She left then, but before long she was back with the orange juice. Mark drank it down quickly, and then she helped him put his robe on. "I'm still thirsty," Mark said.

151

"I'm sure you are. There's a drinking fountain in the day room. Can you stand up for me now?"

Mark got down from the bed, with the nurse supporting him. He pulled away from her, but then he realized that he *was* dizzy. He stood and caught his balance, and she took hold of him around the waist. "Just stand until you feel all right, and then we'll walk. All right?"

"I can walk," Mark said. He wanted her to let go. She was treating him as though he were one of those weirdos in the other beds.

In one corner of the day room was a little room with some worn-out chairs and a television set. Mark's mother was sitting there in a big chair; her head was leaning back and her hair had fallen across the side of her face. The nurse said, "Mrs. Austin," and Mother looked up. Then she stood up abruptly, looking rather disheveled and confused. "Mark wanted to see you for a few minutes."

Mark didn't know what to do. His mother came to him and put her arms around him, but Mark was self-conscious and a little nervous. He stood rather stiffly, not exactly yielding to the embrace. "I'll be close by, if you need me, Mrs. Austin," the nurse said. What did that mean?

Mark sat down on a stiff-backed chair, and his mother sat down opposite him. "Mark, honey, I know this has to be a little strange for you. Did you remember coming here?"

"No. Why didn't they just let me go home? Did I . . . what did I do?"

"Don't you remember what happened on the bus?"

Mark tried to think about that. It seemed terribly distant. "I tried to hurt Whittington—but he was yelling at me and. . . ." Mark remembered trying to tear his face off. Suddenly he felt very nervous again, scared.

"Mark, I think maybe we shouldn't try to talk about that right now. I know you got very upset. The counselor from the school said she talked to you for a while in the afternoon and you were having a lot of trouble thinking straight. I think you've been through an awful lot of stress, honey, but now maybe you can get some help. The doctors here will—"

"No."

"Mark, now don't get excited."

"I'm not staying here. I want to go home. Those guys in there are really weird, Mom."

Tears filled his mother's eyes. "I know, honey. But it won't be for long, I'm sure. You've been holding too much inside you. You just have to work some of these things out."

Mark tried to think what that meant. He was not going to tell anyone—especially not some doctor. He put his hands to the sides of his head. But he knew he had to be careful not to act strange. He suspected the nurse was watching from somewhere.

"Mark, it won't be so bad. You can—"

"Mom, don't." He was trying to think, and she was starting to annoy him. There had to be some other answer, some other way out of this. "I want to go home. And I want to see Willard."

"Mr. Willard?"

"Yes."

"Mark, the doctor won't release you yet, I'm sure. You need to just—"

"I want to see Willard, Mom. It's important." His mother looked confused. Mark tried to calm his voice. "I just want to see him, Mom. It will help me. Honest."

"I think he could come here to visit you, Mark. I'll have to check."

"He went to a hospital this morning—no, yesterday —he might be home now. Would you try to find him?"

"Well, sure, honey. But today you just need to sleep and get yourself feeling rested. Maybe later this week he could come up and see you."

"No, Mom. I want to see him today—or tomorrow, if he can't come today. But soon, okay? Please." His voice was not aggressive or harsh. In fact, he had not spoken to his mother with such softness in a long time.

"All right, Mark. I'll bring him if he can come—and if the doctor says it's okay."

Mark nodded, acceptingly. "It's really important," he said.

The nurse showed up then, and she said that Mark needed to rest, that he shouldn't exert himself. Mark hated her caring tones, so kindly, but the fact was, he *was* tiring and he did want to sleep. When he stood up, his mother tried to hug him again. Mark wanted to respond, but somehow he couldn't. He turned sideways and stood stiffly. His mother kissed him on the cheek. Mark was sorry as she walked away.

"Mom." She turned around, crying. "Will you be here?"

"I'm going home for a while now. But I'll be back. I'll call Mr. Willard."

Mark nodded and started away with the nurse. When they reached his bed, she helped him take his robe off. Mark clung to the back of the hospital gown, and then he sat on the bed. "Did I hurt Whittington?" he asked.

"Who?"

"The kid on the bus."

"No. I don't think so. Not from what I heard. He was only scratched a little."

CHAPTER 16

||||||||||||||||||||||||||||||||||||||||||||||||||||||||||||||||

Mark slept most of the day, and no one bothered him. His mother came to visit him again
that evening. She said that Willard was going to be re-
leased from the hospital he was in the next morning.
She had arranged to pick him up and bring him over
to see Mark. There was not really much to say after
that. Mark had been trying to sort things out in his
head, but he felt tired and unable to focus on any one
idea for very long. Mother only stayed a few minutes,
and then Mark went back to bed.

But he awoke early the next morning, and lying
there in the darkened room, he tried hard to under-

stand what had been going on and what he had to do. He knew he had to do something now—before it was too late—but he had no idea what the answer was. The only thing he knew for sure was that he had to tell someone, that he couldn't keep holding everything inside any longer. And it was just as clear to him that the only person he could tell, at least for now, was Willard. But he was scared—scared to say the words out loud, scared of what Willard might think of him.

After breakfast, the nurse—the one Mark didn't like —came in and said he had a visitor. Mark was dressed now, and he no longer wanted any help. But the nurse went with him. Willard was in the corner where Mom had been. He looked terribly tired and white, and he was wearing an old brown suit that was too big for him. There were only four or five others in the day room, and they were sitting together on the opposite side.

"Are you okay?" Mark asked.

"That's what I was going to ask you," Willard said, and he laughed quietly. "Ain't neither one of us worth much, are we, McGill?" Willard patted him on the shoulder, and Mark smiled a little. Then they both sat down, Willard in the big chair that Mom had sat in the day before. Mark felt self-conscious, nervous. He wasn't at all sure that he wanted to go through with this.

"What did the tests show, Willard?"

"I don't know. I haven't heard yet. But the doctor did say that there really wasn't a whole lot they could do now. It's in my lungs, but it's all through me too."

Mark stared at him. For a time he couldn't think of anything to say. "Willard," he finally said, "I'm sorry about those things I told you."

Willard nodded. Mark could see that Willard's shirt was too big, the collar gathered in under the pull of an old brown tie. He hadn't shaved very well either; there were patches of gray stubble on his neck and around his mouth. "I'm the one that done the wrong thing, Austin. I should've told you sooner, I guess. But that's been a hard thing for me to do. I don't like much to even think about it."

"Are you scared?"

"Yuh, I'm scared." Willard looked down at the tile floor. "I've been scared ever since the doctor first told me what I had. I've seen some of my friends go through so much, you know."

Mark felt tears come into his eyes. He fought them back. But he found himself wishing that he could just let go and cry. A certain tenseness, however, a tightness in his chest and behind his eyes, seemed to be holding him back. "I didn't mean that about the trains," he said.

"Yuh, I know. But I'll say this, Austin, you seen right through me. After I talked to that doctor the first time and he said I had cancer, I went home and did some thinking. That's when I decided to rebuild that train layout before I died. It's the only thing I have that's worth anything, Austin." His voice caught. He sat up a little straighter and tugged at his collar. "But if I was going to fix it up, I had to give it to someone. So I went looking, and I come up with you. What you said about me was exactly right."

"But there's nothing wrong with that, Willard. It's just that when you first said it, it seemed like something my dad would do. It seemed like you were trying to cheat me or something." Mark was surprised—and frightened—by his own words. He sensed that he was seeing certain things that had not been clear to him before. And yet the tenseness was still building. He was tempted to excuse himself and go back to his bed.

"Well, I don't know, Austin. I thought a whole lot about this while I was just laying around in that hospital. I think I can see now what I've been trying to do. I guess I've been trying to leave a piece of me behind. So I wouldn't be quite so dead when I'm dead. That's how scared I am, Austin."

"I'm scared too, Willard." Mark drew all the air he could get into his gripping chest. He and Willard sat looking at each other for some time.

"I'm scared to die—and you're scared to live," Willard said.

They continued to look at each other's eyes until Mark finally had to look down. He had to do it now. He had to tell him. "Willard, I want to talk to you about something." Willard nodded. But Mark felt his fingernails pushing into the palms of his hands, and he felt the tightness rise all the way through his shoulders and up the back of his neck. "I've got to tell someone and—"

"Listen, Austin. They probably have people here at

the hospital who understand things better than I do."
He sounded a little nervous.

"No, I want to tell you." Mark looked past Willard; he stared at the dull green wall, his stomach quivering. "My dad killed himself, Willard."

Willard nodded, his face showing no sign of surprise. "I thought maybe he did," he said.

Mark looked back at the wall. He took a breath. "Willard, it was my fault. He did it because of something I said to him." He felt his stomach grab and his shoulders push forward. Maybe he couldn't do this.

Willard sat quietly for a few seconds. "Are you sure?" he asked.

"Yes." But all these months he had been arguing that point with himself. He wasn't really sure, not entirely.

"What did you say to him, Austin?"

But Mark wasn't ready. Not yet. He tried to swallow and realized how dry his mouth was. "I have to tell you the whole thing, Willard. What happened."

"All right."

"Dad and Mom had been separated for a couple of months, I guess. The divorce still wasn't final. But on that day—when he did it—he came over to our house, and he begged Mom to take him back. He told her he was sorry and that he knew he could change. But Mom didn't believe him." Mark was having a hard time concentrating. He didn't feel that he was making sense. He knew where the story was going, where it had to end up, and he didn't want to get there. "Willard, he used to accuse her of all kinds of things. When he was mad, especially if he had been drinking, he would call her these really terrible names, and he'd accuse her of stepping out with other guys. All kinds of stuff like that. I think it always scared him because she was so pretty. He was scared he would lose her to someone else." Mark had to stop. His voice was shaking. What he had just said was true, and he had known it for a long time, but he had never admitted it before, even to himself.

"Was he really sorry, do you think?"

"Sure, he was sorry. He was always sorry. But he did it over and over again, Willard. And that's what Mom told him. She said she just couldn't ever take him back again."

"I guess I don't blame her, do you?"

"No," Mark said, "I don't." And he meant it, but he knew it had never been that simple in his own mind. "She told him to go away and never come back again. And he started to cry and beg her. Then he said he was going to kill himself." Mark could visualize it, see his dad standing there, the tears running down his face, his hands reaching toward Mother, and she crying too, but holding back. He had seen that moment so many times in his mind, all summer and all fall. He didn't want to have to think about it anymore.

"Did she believe he would do it?"

"I don't think so, Willard." Mark sat for a time. He felt terribly tired. Maybe he couldn't go on with this now. But he also wanted to get it over with. "He told us how he was going to do it, Willard. He said he was going to drive his car into an overpass abutment, out on the freeway. He even told us which one."

"And that's how he did it?"

Mark nodded, and then he put his hands on the sides of his head and tightened his grip, trying to hold his head together. "Mom and I know—and now you do. But no one else does. The police said he fell asleep. They found some skid marks at the very last, just before he hit the abutment. They said he did that when he woke up."

Mark watched Willard. He waited for his response. Things had to be just right if he were going to tell the rest. "Okay, Austin. I see why that ain't easy for you. But it wasn't your fault. Nor your mother's."

"Willard, you still don't know everything. You don't know what I did. I said something to him. Something really bad."

Mark looked carefully at Willard. The old man was squinting as though he were hurting. "You don't need to tell me, Austin. It doesn't matter to me what you said."

That opened it up for Mark. He gripped his fists tight and shoved them into the flesh of his thighs, and then he stared at the floor. "He told me he wanted to take me on a vacation—me and Ronnie—and I told him that I didn't believe him, that I was tired of all his promises that he never kept. So then he left. He went outside, and he was crying, leaning up against the side of his car. I was sorry, Willard. I really was. I *did* want to go on a vacation with him. We had fun together when he wasn't. . . ." Tears had come again, not flowing, but filling Mark's eyes. His voice was hard to control. He fought to keep going. "So I went outside, and I told him I was sorry. But all he did was start all over again. He kept saying that I didn't trust him, that I didn't love him. And he kept saying that Mom had turned me against him. That made me mad, Willard. He was wrong. That was so unfair. Mom was always sticking up for him. And he was so lousy to her. So I got really mad then, and I told him he was nothing but a worthless bum. I told him I hated him. And I *did* hate him, Willard."

Mark pounded his fists on his knees. He wanted to feel angry again. He wanted to feel justified. "The only trouble is," Willard said, "you also loved him, didn't you?"

Mark finally let go and cried. "I miss him, Willard," he said. "I miss him so much." And then he sobbed. Willard reached out and patted him on his knee.

Mark let himself cry for some time, but he was still fighting to say more. He still hadn't said the words. He caught his breath finally, and then he said, "That's still not everything." Now that he had come this far, he had to finish. "He told me what he told Mom—that he was going to kill himself, and he started telling again how he was going to do it." Mark's words were pinched, forced out. "I was so tired of hearing him talk that way, Willard. It was all a big act he always put on to make us feel sorry for him. I lost my temper and I grabbed his jacket. I wanted to do anything to shut him up. I screamed at him. I said. . . ." The sobs came again, and for some time Mark couldn't get the words out. He kept swallowing, trying to get control, until he finally said, "I told him, 'Dad, you don't have the guts to kill yourself.' "

He covered his face then, and he cried more easily. Willard got up and sat down on the chair next to Mark's. He put his arm around Mark's shoulder, but he didn't say anything. Mark knew now that he had wanted to tell this for all these months, and the release really did seem better than what he had been living with. But his mind was still working; he knew the crying didn't take the problem away.

Gradually Mark calmed, and when he could, he said, "So it was my fault, Willard. And I don't know what to do about it."

Willard didn't answer for a long time. He seemed to be thinking very carefully. "Well, Austin," he eventually said, "what he done to you was worse than anything you done to him. He knew exactly what it would do to you when he took your dare like that."

"I know, Willard. I've thought about that a thous-and times. I want to hate him for that—and then maybe I can forget about it. But all I can think of is how much he must have hated me to do it."

Willard didn't respond very quickly again, but when he did, he said, "That ain't the only way to look at it, I guess. Remember the skid marks. At the last, maybe he saw that he was wrong to do it."

"Or I was right about him, Willard."

"In a way, I guess you was. But what I see in your dad, Austin, was an awful lot of weakness—and fear. He was scared—scared to live *and* scared to die." Willard coughed, and then he sat quietly for a time. "He wasn't so different from the rest of us, I guess."

"I know, Willard. He wanted to be a better man. I know he did." Mark began to cry again, but quietly, calmly, not with the earlier anguish.

"Austin," Willard said, still with his arm around Mark's shoulders, "this whole thing ain't a simple matter. What you said to him was wrong, but most people say lots of wrong things in their lives and aren't made to pay for 'em the way you've been paying. They just say they're sorry, and that takes care of it. Your dad got lots of second chances, but he didn't give you even one. That's because he was such a weak man. What you gotta be is stronger. You just have to do it—for your own sake, and for your mother's. You're a good boy, Austin, and the wrongest thing you could do would be to spend the rest of your life thinking you're not."

"I want to be good, Willard. I want to. . . ." He couldn't speak for a time. "I want to feel good inside. But the words keep coming back into my head—the ones I said at the very end. I can't seem to stop thinking about it. I'm scared almost all the time."

Willard patted Mark's shoulder, "Well, Austin, at least all three of us has something in common there. Me and you and your dad. We've all been jamming on the brakes with both feet, ain't we?" Mark didn't say anything, but he was thinking hard. He wanted to feel better; he really did. "I think," Willard said, "that all three of us have spent too much time feeling sorry for ourselves."

Mark tried to think. He was trying to know what the next step should be. "I need to talk to Mom," he finally said.

"That's right, Austin. That's just exactly what you need to do. And then you need to talk to these folks around here that can help you get over this whole thing." Willard stood up, slowly, only gradually straightening out his back. "Damn this old age," he said, chuckling to himself.

He stepped in front of Mark, and then Mark stood up, so the two were facing each other. Mark could see Willard's strong cheekbones, just under the thin skin, and he could see the rich brown of the man's eyes. "Willard, could I still have the trains?"

Tears welled up in Willard's eyes and slid into the creases at the corners. "Sure," he said, and he nodded. "But I ain't finished with 'em quite yet." And then he pulled Mark close and hugged him.